THE

What T
to Be, How They Affect Us

by Alvin Schwartz

Illustrated with photographs

The ..., ..d we are given a look
.. ...ui movement outside this country.
Most important, Mr. Schwartz explains and
illustrates concretely the actual work of
unions: the recruitment of new members; the
negotiation and enforcement of contracts to
improve working conditions and opportunities, wages, benefits, and job security; and
political action to obtain through legislation
what cannot be won by bargaining or striking.

The Unions, which is part of a body of work
on American institutions that includes Mr.
Schwartz's *University,* is lucid in its handling
of concepts and unique in its coverage of the
important events and personalities in American labor relations. Readers will gain from it a
clear understanding of how unions work and
a balanced perspective on the movement as a
whole—its past successes and failures, its pros-
pects for the future.

UNIVERSITY

Alvin Schwartz

Illustrated with photographs

"This is an honest, brightly written account of life
on a large, representative Eastern campus, the
University of Pennsylvania. . . . Young men and
women presently shopping college catalogues will
get a practical, down-to-earth orientation course.

"The author has interviewed dozens of students,
faculty members, chaplains, coaches, and deans at
Penn, then sifted out his impressions in a book
that provides information on practically any question a teen-ager could ask. . . .

"He is particularly strong in areas of social
concern, especially in what he has to say about
the problems of blacks on predominantly white
campuses."   —*The New York Times*

THE
UNIONS

THE UNIONS

What They Are
How They Came to Be
How They Affect Each of Us

ALVIN SCHWARTZ

THE VIKING PRESS | **NEW YORK**

First Edition
Copyright © 1972 by Alvin Schwartz
All rights reserved
First published in 1972 by The Viking Press, Inc.
625 Madison Avenue, New York, N.Y. 10022
Published simultaneously in Canada by
The Macmillan Company of Canada Limited
Library of Congress catalog card number: 70–136827

331.88   1. Labor unions

SBN 670–74098–5

Printed in U.S.A.

1   2   3   4   5   76   75   74   73   72

W 1703428

Illustration Credits

AFL–CIO: 23, 43, 59, 63, 71, 74, 76, 221, 223. AFL–CIO Committee on Political Education: 215, · 218 (top). Amalgamated Clothing Workers of America: 53, 87 (bottom), 99, 169. American Federation of State, County and Municipal Workers: 79, 186. American Institute for Free Labor Development: 231. Associated Press (Wide World Photos): 25, 54, 118, 212. Black Star: 77 (Bob Fitch), 153 (Ted Rozumalski), 208 (Claus C. Meyer). Culver Pictures: 34. *Detroit Free Press–New York Times:* 201. Drug and Hospital Union: 195. Federal Mediation and Conciliation Service: 196. International Association of Machinists and Aerospace Workers: 68, 90, 139. International Chemical Workers Union: 161. International Labour Office: 103. Library of Congress: 39, 41, 46. National Labor Relations Board: 167. National Right to Work Committee: 96 (left). *New York Times:* 84, 192, 218 (bottom). Oklahoma National Association for the Advancement of Colored People: 96 (right). Seafarers International Union: 87 (top). United Automobile, Aerospace, and Agricultural Implement Workers of America: 89, 183, 189. United Press International: 120, 226. United States Department of Labor, Bureau of Labor Statistics: 26, 30, 32–33, 177. United Steelworkers of America: 110.

Contents

PREFACE   9

INTRODUCTION   15

Part One | A MATTER OF CONFLICT   19

1 | Conflict and Local 492   21
2 | The Unions   27
3 | A Look Back   35

Part Two | THE MOVEMENT AND ITS
            MEMBERS   61

4 | The Federation   63
5 | IAM, AFSCME, UFWOC   68
6 | The Internationals   79

7 | The Locals   90
8 | The Rank and File   110
9 | Racketeers and Reformers   120

Part Three | FRIENDS AND ENEMIES   129

10 | Management   131
11 | The Government   135
12 | The Public   143

Part Four | UNIONS AT WORK   151

13 | Organizing the Unorganized   153
14 | Collective Bargaining: The Issues   172
15 | Collective Bargaining: Haggle and Bluff   186
16 | Collective Bargaining: Peace or War?   196
17 | Strike!   201
18 | Politics   212
19 | Unions Abroad   223

Part Five | A LOOK AHEAD   233

CAREERS IN LABOR RELATIONS   239

TERMS USED IN LABOR RELATIONS   245

BIBLIOGRAPHY AND SUGGESTED
  READINGS   251

INDEX   261

Preface

The Unions was prepared over a period of two years. As in any book, the research involved three stages: learning enough to visualize the book, learning enough to organize it in a logical, useful way, and learning enough to ask the questions to obtain the information to write it.

This involved extensive interviewing, usually with a tape recorder, of scores of union members, union officials, workers who were not union members, ordinary citizens, members of management, government officials, and experts in labor–management relations at a number of universities. It also required extensive research in books, government reports, union and employer publications, scholarly journals, and news magazines and daily newspapers. The individuals and organizations on which I relied in my research are listed below with deep gratitude. The publications to which I turned are cited in the bibliography.

INDIVIDUALS AND ORGANIZATIONS
WHICH SERVED AS RESOURCES

AMERICAN FEDERATION OF LABOR–CONGRESS OF INDUSTRIAL ORGANIZATIONS: Walter G. Davis, Nathaniel Goldfinger, C.J. Haggerty, Edward S. Haines, Tom Harris, William L. Kirchner, Joseph Lewis, Michael Mann, Sam Marshall, Rudolph Oswald, Leo Perlis, Henry Santiestevan, Bert Seidman, Don Slaiman, Albert J. Zack, Pat Ziska.

INTERNATIONAL LABOR PRESS ASSOCIATION: Kenneth Fiester.

NEW YORK STATE AFL–CIO: Ludwig Jaffe, Joseph P. Murphy; TEXAS AFL–CIO: Harold Tate.

AMALGAMATED CLOTHING WORKERS OF AMERICA: Burt Beck, Connie Kopolov, Del Mileski; AMALGAMATED LITHOGRAPHERS OF AMERICA, LOCAL 1: Edward Swayduck, Samuel Grafton; AMALGAMATED MEAT CUTTERS AND BUTCHER WORKMEN OF NORTH AMERICA: Ray Dickow, Leslie Orear; AMALGAMATED MEAT CUTTERS, LOCAL 80A: Clarence Clark; AMERICAN FEDERATION OF MUSICIANS: Joe Savage; AMERICAN FEDERATION OF STATE, COUNTY, AND MUNICIPAL WORKERS: Les Finnegan, Thomas Moore McBridge, Donald S. Wasserman; AMERICAN FEDERATION OF TEACHERS (AFT): Dave Elsila; AFT LOCAL 2 (UNITED FEDERATION OF TEACHERS): Vito DeLeonardis, Dan Sanders, Irving Weinstein; AMERICAN NEWSPAPER GUILD: James Cesnik; AMERICAN SOCIETY FOR PROFESSIONAL ENGINEERS: Harold Ammand, Henry J. Andreas.

INTERNATIONAL AIRLINE PILOTS ASSOCIATION: Wallace A. Anderson; INTERNATIONAL ASSOCIATION OF MACHINISTS AND AEROSPACE WORKERS: Paul Burnsky, Gordon H. Cole, William Gomberly; INTERNATIONAL BROTHERHOOD OF TEAMSTERS; INTERNATIONAL LADIES' GARMENT WORKERS' UNION: Leon Stein; INTERNATIONAL UNION OF ELECTRICAL, RADIO, AND MACHINE WORKERS (IUE): Julien Leibner, R.L. Cagnina; IUE LOCAL 492: Harold L. Morrison; MAJOR LEAGUE BASEBALL PLAYERS ASSOCIATION: Richard J. Moss; NATIONAL EDUCATION ASSOCIATION: Rudolph A. Lawton; NEW JERSEY EDUCATION ASSOCIATION: Jack A. Bertelino, Marvin R. Reed; PRINCETON, N.J., REGIONAL EDUCATION ASSOCIATION: Mrs. J.K. Randall.

RETAIL, WHOLESALE, AND DEPARTMENT STORE UNION, LOCAL 1199

(DRUG AND HOSPITAL WORKERS UNION): Moe Foner, Robert Dobbs, Marshall Dubin; SEAFARERS INTERNATIONAL UNION OF NORTH AMERICA: Irving Spivack; TEXTILE WORKERS UNION OF AMERICA: Irving Kahan, Paul Swaity; TRANSPORT WORKERS UNION OF AMERICA (TWUA); TWUA LOCAL 550 (AIRLINE STEWARDS AND STEWARDESSES ASSOCIATION): Helen Chase.

UNITED AUTOMOBILE, AEROSPACE, AND AGRICULTURAL IMPLEMENT WORKERS OF AMERICA (UAW): Alvin Adams, William L. Hardy, Ray Martin, Ralph D. Robinson, Joseph Walsh; UAW LOCAL 502: Fred Mann; UAW LOCAL 731: James Gazzarro; UNITED BROTHERHOOD OF CARPENTERS AND JOINERS OF AMERICA, LOCAL 781: William H. Fry; UNITED FARM WORKERS ORGANIZING COMMITTEE: Delores Huerta, Fred Ross; UNITED MINE WORKERS OF AMERICA: Justin McCarthy; UNITED STEELWORKERS OF AMERICA: Bruce Alexander, Richard Miller, Donald Smith; UNITED TRANSPORTATION UNION: L.E. Cori.

AFRO-AMERICAN LABOR COUNCIL: David Brembart, Irving Brown, Naomi Spatz, Lester Trachtman; AMERICAN INSTITUTE FOR FREE LABOR DEVELOPMENT: Angelo Verdu; INTERNATIONAL CONFEDERATION OF FREE TRADE UNIONS: T. Barry-Braunthal; INTERNATIONAL LABOUR ORGANIZATION: Rudolph Faupl (U.S. Worker Delegate), W.J. Knight.

A. PHILIP RANDOLPH INSTITUTE: Norman Hill; ASSOCIATION OF CATHOLIC TRADE UNIONISTS; JEWISH LABOR COMMITTEE: Martin Lapan; LEAGUE FOR INDUSTRIAL DEMOCRACY: Judy Bardacke, Max Green, Rochelle Horowitz; WORKERS DEFENSE LEAGUE: Robert Joe Pierpont.

GENERAL ELECTRIC COMPANY: Henry Bachrach; PRINCETON, N.J., REGIONAL SCHOOLS BOARD OF EDUCATION: H.D. Rothberg; UNION CARBIDE CORPORATION: William Atkinson; UNITED STATES STEEL CORPORATION: Donald Clay, J. Warren Shaver.

CHAMBER OF COMMERCE OF THE UNITED STATES: Joseph M. Gambatese; NATIONAL ASSOCIATION OF MANUFACTURERS: Phyllis H. Moehrle; NATIONAL RIGHT TO WORK COMMITTEE: Reed Larson.

FEDERAL MEDIATION AND CONCILIATION SERVICE: Norman Walker; NATIONAL LABOR RELATIONS BOARD: George Bokat, Clement P. Cull, Iliff McMahan, Elihu Platt; AGENCY FOR INTERNATIONAL DEVELOPMENT: John M. McGonagle; U.S. DEPARTMENT OF

LABOR: Charles A. Caldwell, Patrick H. Gannon, Tommy C. Ishee, John W. Leslie; U.S. SENATE COMMITTEE ON LABOR AND PUBLIC WELFARE; U.S. SENATE COMMITTEE ON GOVERNMENT OPERATIONS.

AMERICAN ARBITRATION ASSOCIATION: Tia Dennenberg, Mary Jo Douds, Morris Stone; CENTER FOR THE STUDY OF DEMOCRATIC INSTITUTIONS; CITIZENS RESEARCH FOUNDATION: Herbert E. Alexander; INSTITUTE OF COLLECTIVE BARGAINING AND GROUP RELATIONS; NATIONAL ORGANIZATION OF WOMEN LEGAL DEFENSE FUND: Grace D. Cox; PURDUE OPINION PANEL, PURDUE UNIVERSITY.

THE NEW YORK STATE SCHOOL OF INDUSTRIAL AND LABOR RELATIONS, CORNELL UNIVERSITY: Alice Cook, Jerry Brown, Donald P. Dietrich, Ronald Donovan, Wayne Hodges, Vernon Jenson, Dorothy Nelkin, John Windmuller; EDUCATIONAL FILM LIBRARY ASSOCIATION: Esme Cook, Barbara VanDyke; RUTGERS UNIVERSITY LABOR EDUCATION CENTER: Norman Eigar; RUTGERS UNIVERSITY SCHOOL OF LIBRARY SCIENCE: Elaine Simpson, Phyllis VanOrden; PRINCETON, N.J. REGIONAL SCHOOLS; HAMILTON TOWNSHIP, N.J. REGIONAL SCHOOLS.

LIBRARIES AT BOWDOIN COLLEGE; PRINCETON UNIVERSITY: Helen Fairbanks; RUTGERS UNIVERSITY: Bernard Downey; THE EDUCATIONAL TESTING SERVICE; THE NATIONAL INDUSTRIAL CONFERENCE BOARD; THE PRINCETON, N.J., PUBLIC LIBRARY.

ATTITUDE SURVEY

Since I hoped large numbers of young people would read this book, my research also involved them. As workers and managers of the future, how much did they know about the unions, and what were their attitudes toward them? To gain a sense of where they stood, I conducted a survey among 120 juniors and seniors at high schools in Hamilton Township, New Jersey, a working-class community with many union members, and Princeton, New Jersey, primarily a residence for business executives, university professors, and other professionals. Students completed detailed questionnaires as part of their social studies classes. Although those at Hamilton tended to show somewhat more sympathy for unionism, curiously they knew no more about the labor movement than their counterparts in Princeton.

Introduction

When I was in high school I knew practically nothing about the labor movement. One of my few sources of information was my father. Although he was a union member, he thought unions were run by a lot of irresponsible hotheads he wished would leave him alone. But other than that he had little to say on the subject.

My high-school teachers also had little to offer. The only exception was the man who taught American history, but what intrigued him was not social injustice or the theory of the working class but the bloody warfare that erupted in the 1870s when workers tried to form unions and big business tried to discourage them. Nor were my teachers in college particularly interested in the labor movement, although by then I was. Nor today are my friends, who otherwise are well informed. Nor are the newspapers and magazines I rely on.

Like my old history teacher, what fascinates them are strikes and little more.

Why we do not know more or care more about unions is a puzzle. In many cases they are the only practical means we have of protecting ourselves against injustices in our jobs. But whether or not we are union members, unions affect our wages, the conditions under which we work, and the conditions under which we live. The more I have read about the labor movement and the more I have talked with unionists, businessmen, and scholars, the clearer it has become that when we study unions we study ourselves. It is what makes the subject so important and so intriguing.

—Alvin Schwartz

Who is on my side? Who?
2 KINGS 9:32

Part One | A MATTER OF CONFLICT

Scholars tell us that conflict between labor and management is inevitable, that it will persist as long as there are workers and managers. It is rooted, they say, in the age-old clash between the "haves" and the "have nots." But it also grows from a fundamental clash of goals. Workers want job security and fair treatment. Managers want freedom to make their organizations more efficient and more profitable. When a manager's decisions threaten a worker's job, the worker resists. When a worker's demands threaten a manager's freedom, the manager resists. In a dictatorship the government settles these clashes. In a democracy the parties themselves do, which is why we have unions and collective bargaining and, at times, strikes.

1 | Conflict and Local 492

Except for a few clerks and supervisors, the light-bulb factory in Newark was empty. But around the corner the former meat market where Local 492 had its headquarters was jammed with workers. Each Monday morning at ten they came to the strike meeting to learn the latest news, collect their twenty dollars from the strike fund, pick up any food other unions had left for them, and have a cup of coffee.

When the checks and the food had been distributed that morning and the coffee had been poured, Harold Morrison, the local's president, climbed up on an old chopping block to give his weekly report and pep talk. Negotiations still were deadlocked, he told the strikers, and there still was a need to be patient, but there was no need to be pessimistic. "We are going to go back only when *we* want to!" he shouted, to which everyone cheered. Two students from Rutgers University then presented the union with $111 they had collected to help with the strike. "Next week we will have more," one said. "The students are with you!" The woman in charge of the Welfare Committee then asked those strikers who were short of money to see her. And the meeting adjourned.

In front of the light-bulb factory twenty men and women walked a picket line in the biting cold. Hugging themselves to keep warm, they trudged along the snow-covered sidewalk for about a hundred feet, then retraced their steps, then started out again. When they got tired, they retreated to a rented trailer the union kept nearby where there were a heater and a pot of coffee.

The strike had begun three months earlier when the General Electric Company and the fourteen unions that represented its workers could not agree on a new contract. The day the old contract expired 130,000 men and women, including 500 in Newark, walked off the job. The major issue was money. With inflation driving up the cost of living, the unions were insisting on a large raise. But the company maintained its original offer was fair, that its production and earnings did not permit any more of an increase. After ninety days, however, what was "fair" and what was not was irrelevant. There was only one question. Could the workers hold out long enough to force the company to improve its offer? While Local 492 met in Newark that morning, negotiators for the company and the fourteen national unions met in New York with government mediators. But once again there was no progress toward a settlement.

Ninety days is a long time to be without pay. In Newark the strikers and their families were not eating well, nor were

Striking General Electric workers boycott a
Boston department store that sells GE products.

they buying clothing or other things they needed, but they were getting by. There was the twenty dollars they received each week from the strike fund. In addition, some had savings or relatives to rely on. Others had found temporary jobs at the post office or in one of the department stores. In addition, a few with large families were getting welfare payments.

Without the dues their members ordinarily paid, the fourteen national unions also had financial problems. Strike benefits and other expenses came to almost a million dollars a week, and their reserves were shrinking. To help meet these costs, other unions had contributed more than $3 million, but whether this would be enough only time would tell. To increase the pressure on General Electric they also had organized a national boycott. In Baltimore, Chicago, Cleveland, and other cities, thousands of unionists picketed department stores, urging shoppers not to buy GE products until the strike was over.

But the company fought back. Each week it purchased one or more full-page advertisements in newspapers across the country in which it presented its side of the dispute. Each week the company also sent every striker a letter in which it urged that he return to work. The latest letter to the strikers in Newark reported that 1500 workers had abandoned the strike and gone back to their jobs at the company's other light-bulb plants. "If you are at all hesitant [about returning]," the letter said, ". . . get a few of your friends together to come in with you." The company's supervisors were also visiting workers at their homes to persuade them to return. But in Newark, at least, they had no takers.

After ninety days the members of Local 492 still were convinced they would win a better contract. "We are backing them into a corner," one said. "It is just a matter of time," another explained. Whether they were right remained to be seen. The company still had a large inventory of products it had assembled before the strike. In addition, a number of plants where workers had not struck were in operation. But the strike had cut the company's production by 70 per cent and, as a result, had sharply reduced its earnings. As a result of the boycott, moreover, fewer persons were buying GE products. But whether all this hurt enough to force concessions was something only the company knew.

In Newark only the workers, their families, and the company were seriously affected by the strike. But in cities in which General Electric was a major employer it was a different story. In Schenectady, New York, where the company had 12,000 employees, one worker in four was idle. With the weekly payroll cut by millions of dollars, local businessmen suffered severe losses. Business firms elsewhere also were affected. Many that supplied GE with materials closed down. So did others that relied on GE parts for products they pro-

Pickets at a GE plant in Schenectady, New York, keep nonstrikers from their jobs.

duced. The result was that thousands of men and women not involved in the strike also were out of work.

A man without work has two big problems. One, as we have seen, is money. The other is filling the time he suddenly has. In Newark some strikers spent their time on union business. They served on the Strike Committee, which dealt with strategy; the Negotiating Committee, which bargained over local working conditions; the Kitchen Committee, which fed those on strike duty; or the Welfare Committee. At night they visited other local unions in the area to raise more money for the strike. But most of the strikers had little to do after they put in their time on the picket line. They looked for temporary jobs, or fixed up their houses, or went hunting or played with their children. Or they merely waited and wondered.

MILLIONS OF MEMBERS

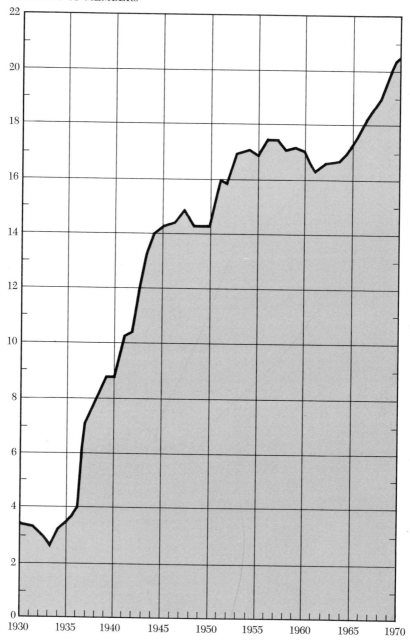

2 | The Unions

More than 20 million Americans in every industry and craft and in a growing number of professions are union members. They belong to 80,000 local unions in cities and towns across the country. In turn, these locals make up 200 "international unions." [*] And two thirds of these make up the AFL–CIO, the American Federation of Labor–Congress of Industrial Organizations, which speaks for labor on the national scene. These millions of workers, their unions, and their federation are the labor movement.

1 All international unions are power centers through which

---

[*] The term *international* is used because most unions have at least a few lo-cals in Canada or Puerto Rico, along with those in the United States. How-ever, unions without such locals also describe themselves as internationals.

workers try to win improvements in their jobs they could not hope to win alone./Moreover, all rely on the same methods. One is collective bargaining with employers over wages, hours, and working conditions. The other is political action to obtain through laws what cannot be won through bargaining. Most also are deeply involved in recruiting new members and organizing new locals to increase their strength and bargaining power.

One quickly learns, however, that unions differ markedly. There are, for example, giant unions like the Teamsters, the Auto Workers, and the Steelworkers with over a million members, hundreds of local unions, and staffs of over a thousand.° But there also are unions like the Watch Workers, the Window Cutters, and the Cigar Makers, which have only a few thousand members.

There are craft unions, like the Carpenters and the Plumbers, which restrict their membership to workers with a particular skill. There also are industrial unions, like the Rubber Workers, which recruit everyone from factory hands to office clerks. There are unions which have fully organized the occupations or industries with which they deal. Thus, every airline pilot carries a union card and so do almost every actor and almost every barber. But other unions like the Textile Workers and the Farm Workers devote most of their efforts and resources to organizing the unorganized, often in the face of severe opposition from employers.

There are many unions which are concerned only with negotiating contracts and handling their members' complaints about conditions on the job. But some work not only to im-

---

° Officially they are the International Brotherhood of Teamsters, Chauffeurs, Warehousemen, and Helpers of America; the United Automobile, Aerospace, and Agricultural Implement Workers of America; and the United Steelworkers of America.

prove wages, but to improve the lives of their members. The Auto Workers, for example, operate a major education center and vacation resort. The Ladies' Garment Workers' provide a chain of health clinics. The Amalgamated Clothing Workers sponsor housing projects and, with employers, maintain child-care centers where members can leave their children while they are at work.

There are many unions which have excellent relationships with employers and rarely find it necessary to strike. But others are so in conflict with management that the two sides seem like opposing armies.

The character of a union is determined to an important extent by its leaders. Sidney Hillman of the Clothing Workers and Walter Reuther of the Auto Workers helped create organizations that made major contributions to the nation's welfare. James Hoffa of the Teamsters, who spent four years behind bars for his corrupt activities, had an opposite effect. But over the long term the nature of a union inevitably is shaped by its members and their problems.

About 40 per cent of the union members in this country are craftsmen and factory workers, men and women who produce goods. For many years they dominated the labor movement, but this is no longer the case. The majority of union members now are "gray collar," white collar, and professional workers who perform services. It is a group that has been steadily expanding since the 1950s. Among others, it includes store clerks, office clerks, hospital workers, waiters, bartenders, insurance agents, repairmen, technicians, policemen, sanitation workers, teachers, librarians, welfare workers, musicians, and major league baseball players. As a result of this change, a new kind of labor movement has been taking shape. Its members are better educated and more skilled than those in the past. They also are more representative of the many kinds of workers in this country.

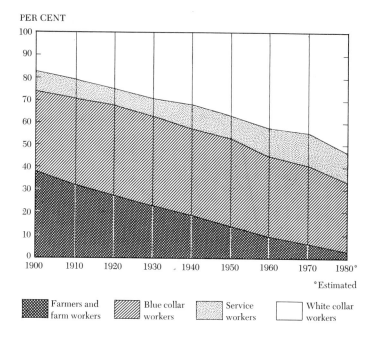

PER CENT

Farmers and farm workers   Blue collar workers   Service workers   White collar workers

Changes in the nature of the work force from 1900 through the 1970s.

In theory, every international union represents the workers in a particular occupation or industry, which it regards as its exclusive "jurisdiction." In practice, many unions move into new fields whenever the opportunity presents itself. The Seafarers International Union, for example, includes not only seamen and fishermen, but cannery workers and taxi drivers. The Steelworkers union operates not only in the steel industry, but in the aluminum, copper, and can industries. It also has members who make lawn mowers, nail-file clippers, golf clubs and major league baseball bats. The Teamsters union is the nation's most diverse. Its original members were truck drivers, descendants of the men who hauled loads with teams of horses. Now the union regards as a potential member anyone who depends on products carried by trucks, which takes in virtually everyone. Today there are Teamsters in the airline, automotive, baking, chemical, construction, food, furniture, lumber, newspaper, printing, rubber, and warehousing industries, among others.

As one result, there is a growing number of large general unions in the United States. The Teamsters, Auto Workers, Steelworkers, Machinists, and Electrical Workers together represent a third of all the union members in this country. As another result, many unions now compete for members in the same industry or occupation. Frequently workers must choose from among several unions that wish to represent them (see chapter 13).

However, only a minority of workers in the United States have union cards. Of the 80 million people in the work force when this was written, about 25 per cent were union members. If farm workers, who are largely unorganized, are excluded, union members represent 28 per cent of the work force. By contrast, in many European countries 40 to 70 per cent of the workers are in unions (see chapter 19).

Despite its relatively small size the labor movement has been responsible for many important changes in our lives. Through bargaining with employers, unions have achieved a major redistribution of the nation's wealth. They have won for their members the highest wages and most extensive system of benefits in the world, gains which also have influenced the earnings of nonunion workers. These improvements have reduced poverty, brought many workers into the middle class, and made possible the development of mass markets on which modern business depends.

The unions also have achieved a major redistribution of power. Before the spread of unionism in the 1930s most employees had little influence on the conditions under which they worked or on the wages they were paid. If an employer decided to cut wages, increase hours, or transfer a worker to

UNION MEMBERSHIP BY STATES IN 1970 °

	Approximate membership	State ranking	Percentage of all workers	State ranking
ALABAMA †	204,000	24	20.3	29
ALASKA	25,000	47	27.1	19
ARIZONA †	96,000	31	17.6	36
ARKANSAS †	95,000	32	17.9	33
CALIFORNIA	2,137,000	2	30.5	14
COLORADO	152,000	27	20.5	28
CONNECTICUT	290,000	17	24.2	22
DELAWARE	48,000	42	22.6	24
FLORIDA †	299,000	16	13.9	46
GEORGIA †	251,000	19	16.2	42
HAWAII	82,000	35	28.1	17
IDAHO	38,000	45	18.5	30
ILLINOIS	1,548,000	4	35.7	8
INDIANA	657,000	8	35.6	9
IOWA †	186,000	26	21.1	25
KANSAS †	112,000	30	16.6	40
KENTUCKY	250,000	20	27.3	18
LOUISIANA	193,000	25	18.4	31
MAINE	61,000	41	18.4	32
MARYLAND— DISTRICT OF COLUMBIA	463,000	13	23.3	23
MASSACHUSETTS	573,000	10	25.6	21
MICHIGAN	1,195,000	6	40.2	2
MINNESOTA	378,000	15	28.9	16
MISSISSIPPI †	76,000	37	13.2	47
MISSOURI	594,000	9	35.9	7
MONTANA	73,000	39	36.4	5
NEBRASKA †	86,000	34	17.9	34

another job or fire him, short of a strike there was nothing to stop him from doing so. However, most unionized workers now have a strong voice in such matters.

As unions have grown stronger they also have increased their political power. Many officeholders owe their election to financial contributions and other support labor gives its friends, and many important laws are largely the result of pressures exerted by the labor movement. These range from workmen's compensation, which provides benefits for inju-

	Approximate membership	State ranking	Percentage of all workers	State ranking
NEVADA †	66,000	40	32.8	11
NEW HAMPSHIRE	45,000	43	17.3	37
NEW JERSEY	768,000	7	29.5	15
NEW MEXICO	43,000	44	14.8	44
NEW YORK	2,555,000	1	35.6	10
NORTH CAROLINA †	137,000	28	7.8	50
NORTH DAKOTA †	28,000	46	17.2	38
OHIO	1,413,000	5	36.3	6
OKLAHOMA	124,000	29	16.1	43
OREGON	218,000	23	30.7	13
PENNSYLVANIA	1,617,000	3	37.2	4
RHODE ISLAND	89,000	33	26.1	20
SOUTH CAROLINA †	81,000	36	9.6	49
SOUTH DAKOTA †	21,000	49	11.9	48
TENNESSEE †	274,000	18	20.6	27
TEXAS †	523,000	11	14.4	45
UTAH †	75,000	38	20.9	26
VERMONT	24,000	48	16.2	41
VIRGINIA †	245,000	21	16.7	39
WASHINGTON	434,000	14	40.0	3
WEST VIRGINIA	221,000	22	43.0	1
WISCONSIN	482,000	12	31.4	12
WYOMING †	19,000	50	17.7	35

° Agricultural employees not included.
† States with "right to work laws," legislation which tends to reduce union membership. See chapter 7.

ries on the job, to legislation to reduce poverty, eliminate discrimination, and improve housing and health care.

With its deep commitment to change, the labor movement inevitably has become one of the nation's most controversial institutions. It is not surprising, therefore, that a great many people tend to regard themselves either as prolabor or antilabor. But such sweeping judgments are unfortunate. For if one is thoughtful it is hard to be completely for or against any movement that includes 200 separate national organizations and more than 20 million men and women from all walks of life.

An early Labor Day parade at Union Square in New York.

3 | A Look
| Back

The history of the American labor movement is the history of millions upon millions of men and women with no money and little education who over a period of two hundred years organized unions that brought them better treatment and a degree of dignity in their work. They succeeded despite extraordinary opposition by their employers, the police, the courts, the press, and public opinion. When they tried to organize unions, they were spied upon, fired from their jobs, and blacklisted from other jobs. Some were jailed. Others were attacked, even killed. At times they succeeded in organizing unions only to see them beaten down by employers or destroyed by fear of reprisal or by an economic depression. Often years would elapse before a new union would emerge from the wreckage of past attempts. And of these only some would survive.

As one reads the accounts of this long, frustrating struggle, then considers the size and power of the labor movement today, and the wages and working conditions we take for granted, it is hard to believe that all this happened. Yet the struggle to form unions still goes on.[*]

STIRRINGS

The first unionists in this country were shoemakers, weavers, carpenters, printers, and other journeymen in the skilled trades. Before the Revolutionary War they formed "sick-and-visiting societies," "death-and-benefit societies," and other organizations to help one another in time of trouble. After the war they began to concern themselves increasingly with economic matters, for their status was changing. In the past they had trained under master craftsmen preparing themselves for the day when they would have their own shops. But as new markets developed and the demand for goods soared, the master craftsman became a large-scale supplier, the journeyman became just another employee, and his chance of starting a business all but disappeared. With the longer hours he had to work and the lower pay he received, his discontent grew.

And with discontent came unions. The first were temporary organizations. When a problem arose the journeymen affected banded together to deal with it, then disbanded

---

[*] Only the most pertinent events in this long history are covered in this chapter. But the full story of the labor movement and the men and women who shaped it is a fascinating example of what ordinary people can achieve if they must. For the many good books that deal at length with this subject, see the Bibliography and Suggested Readings.

when it was settled. It was not until 1794, in Washington's second administration, that the cordwainers, or shoemakers, in Philadelphia organized what would become the nation's first relatively permanent union, the Federal Society of Journeyman Cordwainers. For a fifty-cent initiation fee and dues of about a nickel a month, any journeyman cordwainer in the city could join. However, he agreed not to work in the same shop with a nonunion cordwainer. He also vowed not to work for less than a union wage. To make certain that the members kept their vow, a "tramping committee," the equivalent of today's union business agent, regularly visited the shops where they worked.

A printer's union was organized in New York about the same time and soon other craft unions appeared. However, success was temporary. In 1806 a Philadelphia court ruled that unions were illegal conspiracies to restrain trade. But even unions that ignored the ruling failed when two economic depressions devastated the nation. It was not until prosperity returned late in the 1820s that small craft unions again appeared in sizable numbers. To help in recruiting members and in striking, they organized small local federations, "city centrals," which turned to politics when bargaining with employers proved fruitless and larger problems arose.

In Philadelphia they formed the Workingmen's Party—the Workies—the world's first political organization that represented the interests of workers. As many as sixty other workingmen's parties appeared throughout the country, all seeking a ten-hour day, free public schools, and an end to imprisonment for debt. (Four prisoners in five in Boston, New York, and other cities were serving sentences for nonpayment of debts, most of which were under twenty dollars.) A small national labor federation also was organized, the National Trades Union Council. But another depression, the Panic of 1837, destroyed half the nation's jobs and decimated the fledgling movement.

By 1842 when the Massachusetts Supreme Court declared that unions indeed were legal, many workers had turned their backs on industry and the unions. Some had headed west to start life anew. Others had joined cooperatives where workers owned the means of production, produced goods for sale, and shared the earnings. But when scores of these failed and industry again revived, so did the unions. As the Civil War approached there were in all perhaps a hundred local unions in Boston, New York, Philadelphia, and Baltimore. A number of small international unions also had been formed, including the Hat Finishers, the Stone Cutters, the Locomotive Engineers, and two that to this day remain in operation, the Iron Molders and the Typographers. When the war came and industry expanded, jobs increased and unions grew. In the major cities the number of local unions more than doubled and the number of union members rose toward 200,000, virtually all of whom were craftsmen.

While skilled cordwainers struggled to support themselves early in the century with handcrafted shoes, unskilled workers were turning out ordinary footwear in far greater quantities. Few could make a shoe on their own, but in the small factories where they worked the task was divided into simple steps and each worker performed but one. Other factories were turning out textiles in the same way. In Rhode Island, in fact, a transplanted Englishman named Samuel Slater operated a mill that produced cloth automatically on looms driven by water power.

The division of labor and the introduction of machinery made it possible to produce a growing volume and variety of

Workers at a textile mill in
Lawrence, Massachusetts, in the 1860s.
Drawing by Winslow Homer.

goods at lower prices, which was an important step forward. But in the name of progress, an increasing number of workers were putting in long hours at simple-minded drudgery under the worst of conditions for the poorest wages. A steadily growing number were journeymen in the handicrafts, particularly cordwainers and weavers, whose jobs had been eliminated by the new methods. But many others were women and children. By 1820 half the factory workers in the United States were under eleven years of age and some were as young as four. No matter what his age, however, a factory hand worked fourteen hours a day every day except Sunday. For this a man received a dollar a day, a woman half that amount or less, and a child but seven or eight cents.

By 1850 there were over 3000 textile mills in operation along with uncounted factories and workshops that produced shoes, nails, iron pipe, clocks, sewing machines, firearms, and scores of other products. Here and there strikes erupted. But unlike the journeymen, most factory workers did not strike and did not form unions. Without tools, skills, money, or other jobs to turn to, how could it be otherwise?

THE GILDED AGE

The end of the Civil War saw a dramatic expansion of the Industrial Revolution in the United States. It also marked the beginning of our urban society as workers crowded into cities and towns to take jobs in newly expanding industries. Mark Twain ironically called this period the gilded age. Now industry, railroads, construction, and mining spread across the face of the land. In the process, giant corporations emerged owned by financiers in distant cities who thought of workers not as individuals but as "labor," an expendable commodity to be purchased for the lowest possible sum.

Although jobs differed from industry to industry, everywhere in the 1860s and 1870s hours were long, conditions were dismal, and wages were at rock bottom, driven down by a continuing flood of immigrants willing to work for next to nothing. Yet few workers had the means to escape and most knew better than to complain. Like characters in a Greek tragedy, workers and owners moved toward inevitable conflict. Unable to improve their lives, trapped in an intolerable situation, more and more workers thought in terms of a union to win their rights. Determined to build their companies, the owners stood ready to crush whoever interfered. Armed guards protected their property. Spies checked on their workers. And troublemakers who were found out were fired and blacklisted from other jobs. But as the years wore on, discontent could not always be controlled.

In July 1877, in the midst of still another depression marked by widespread unemployment, forty brakemen and firemen on the Baltimore & Ohio Railroad walked off the job. The company had cut their pay 10 per cent after earlier cutting it 25 per cent. But management would not discuss the matter, and although they had no union the workers

Strikers clash with Federal troops in Baltimore during the nationwide railroad strike of 1877. Drawing by Winslow Homer.

struck. Overnight the unplanned strike spread throughout the entire system. In a matter of days workers on eight other lines whose wages also had been cut joined the strike, halting rail traffic throughout most of the country.

In Baltimore, Chicago, St. Louis, San Francisco, and other cities, strikers demonstrated against their employers. When unemployed workers from other industries joined them, the demonstrations frequently grew into major riots in which railroad and other property was destroyed. Pittsburgh was terrorized for three days by such outbreaks and Chicago was in turmoil for a week. Over 20,000 Federal troops finally brought the disturbances to a halt, but not before a hundred persons had been killed, hundreds more had been injured, and tens of millions of dollars in damage had been done, and all in vain.

The strike against the railroads marked the beginning of an ugly conflict between workers and employers that would persist for generations. Again and again frustration over poor treatment and demands for a share of the gains of industrialization burst into violence. There were bitter strikes in the coal fields of Pennsylvania and Colorado, in the silver mines in Idaho, in the textile mills at Fall River, Massachusetts, in the steel mill at Homestead, Pennsylvania, and in scores of other places. For the first time the nation became aware of labor's frustrations. But the workers themselves won little other than a growing sense of solidarity and an increasing desire for power.

UNIONISM PURE AND SIMPLE

On a cold winter's night in 1869 nine idealistic garment cutters in Philadelphia established what would become the nation's first major labor organization. They called it the Noble and Holy Order of the Knights of Labor. One of their goals was to unite all workers in one big union. Another was to replace the capitalistic system and the low wages it provided. Instead they visualized a system of cooperatives in which workers, with government help, would own the means of production and share whatever was earned. They also sought the eight-hour day, an end to child labor, equal pay for women, and many other social reforms. To achieve all this they would educate the public and change the laws. Only as a last resort would they turn to bargaining with employers and to strikes.

What contributed most to their success, however, was that almost anyone could become a member: skilled craftsmen, unskilled workers who up to then had no unions, black workers, women, and also small businessmen and farmers.

Entire local unions, even national unions, could join. Only bankers, lawyers, stockholders, and gamblers were barred. To protect its members from being fired and blacklisted, the organization at first was a secret society with its own code, handshake, and mystic symbol. But when this approach was discarded it began a period of remarkable growth.

By 1885 the Knights had acquired 100,000 members, a third of all the nation's unionists. And when events forced a strike against the railroad empire of financier Jay Gould, and

For many years children like these coal miners worked as long and hard as adults, a situation early unions fought but did not have the power to correct.

Gould granted all the Knights' demands, workers flocked to their standard. Within a year the organization had grown to 700,000 members. Having reached this pinnacle, however, it began an equally remarkable decline.

The Knights had many problems which contributed to their fall, but the most critical was a split in their membership. For years their craft unions had bridled over the emphasis on cooperatives, social uplift, and education of the public. What they wanted were higher wages, shorter hours, bargaining, and strikes, not utopian designs for the future. They also wanted an organization that emphasized their problems, not those of unskilled workers with whom they felt nothing in common. But when none of this came to pass, in 1886 the craft unions left the Knights and, with a number of other unions, formed the American Federation of Labor. As their first president they selected a hardheaded realist who had no interest in utopia, an English immigrant named Samuel Gompers, president of the Cigar Makers.

The new organization differed from the Knights in many ways. Instead of one big union, it was a loose federation of national unions. Instead of members of all kinds, its members were restricted to skilled craftsmen. Unskilled Mine Workers and Garment Workers soon would join them, but for many years they would be the exceptions. The federation also was not interested in abolishing wages or changing the economic system in other ways. Its only concern, in Gompers's words, was "pure and simple unionism." All it wanted for its members was more money and better conditions, which it would seek through bargaining and strikes.

By 1900 the AFL included forty-eight national unions with over a half million members. The Knights by then were dead. For the time being so was the hope of the great mass of unskilled workers for unions to represent them. But fed by their discontent and frustration, other currents were running strong.

DOWN INTO THE GUTTER

"Fellow workers! This is the Continental Congress of the working class. We are here to confederate the workers of this country into a working class movement . . . to put the working class in possession of economic power . . . [and] in control of the machinery of production. . . ." *

The speaker was "Big Bill" Haywood, one-eyed leader of the ultraradical Western Federation of Miners. The place was Brand's Hall, Chicago. The year was 1905. In the audience were two hundred labor radicals from all over the country who for years had tried without success to mobilize a working-class movement that would exert the power its numbers seemed to warrant. They had come to Chicago to establish a new labor federation which would organize the unskilled workers in whom the AFL and its unions had shown no interest. Out of ten days of debate emerged the Industrial Workers of the World, the Wobblies, as they became known.

"We are going down into the gutter," Haywood declared, "to get at the mass of workers and bring them up to a decent plane of living." The goal, as it was with the Knights of Labor, was "one big union" to which workers of every kind would belong. But another Wobbly goal was "one big strike" through which ultimately workers would seize the means of production and put an end to capitalism. The Wobblies worked to form unions everywhere. No group was too small or too remote to help, with the result that tens of thousands

---

* Thomas R. Brooks, *Toil and Trouble* (New York: Delacorte Press, 1964).

*A rally of Wobblies and other radical labor groups
at Union Square in New York in the early 1900s.*

of workers in lumber camps, wheat fields, seaports, mines, mills, and breweries, many of them migrant workers, acquired the small red cards that made them members.

Since the Wobblies wanted to destroy capitalism, not live in harmony with it, they rejected collective bargaining, relying instead on direct action, a tactic borrowed from European revolutionaries. When workers were mistreated or their demands for improvements were not met, Wobbly organizers led them in strikes, boycotts, even sabotage. When confronted with violence and at times murder, members of the organization responded with violence and murder. To fan the flames of discontent they proclaimed their ideas from street corners in cities and towns across the country.

During a dozen years the Wobblies led almost 150 strikes and acquired possibly 100,000 members, but they built few lasting unions. Rebellion was more their line. But through their example they demonstrated for the first time that unskilled industrial workers could be organized and win victories.

Soon after the United States entered World War I, the Federal government cracked down on the nation's radicals out of fear that they would undermine the war effort. Federal agents arrested thousands of Wobblies, closed their union halls, and confiscated their records and propaganda. The organization never regained its power, but it refused to die. In 1970 on the Berkeley campus of the University of California, fifty students formed a new chapter. When this was written, the Industrial Workers of the World still was listed by the Attorney General of the United States as a subversive organization.

BUSINESS AS USUAL

When the First World War started, the AFL had 2.5 million members. By the time the war ended, its membership had risen to 5 million as a result of the government's efforts to promote labor–management peace and keep war production high. But with the end of the war, business launched a vigorous counterattack. Company after company refused to deal with the unions that had been formed with government help and savagely repelled efforts to organize new unions.

Armed guards, labor spies, blacklists, and strikebreakers all reappeared. So did a legal device called a "yellow dog" contract, through which a worker, in return for a job, agreed not to join a union. A number of employers also took a new tack. To discourage unionism, for the first time they provided insurance programs, pension plans, and recreational facilities for their employees. A great many also formed "company unions," which gave employees a limited voice in their jobs. At one point these unions had a million and a half members.

In 1924 Samuel Gompers died after heading the AFL for thirty-seven years. William Green of the United Mine Workers replaced him, but did little to revive labor's diminishing power. His major program was aimed at improving cooperation with businesses, but business, needless to say, was not interested. By 1929 union membership had shrunk to 3.5 million members, or 6 per cent of the work force. Almost everywhere labor was in retreat.

TURNABOUT

During the 1920s thousands of companies and millions of individuals consistently lived beyond their means, borrowing heavily from banks and speculating to an extraordinary degree in business ventures and stocks. On October 24, 1929— Black Thursday, as it became known—their greed caught up with them. On that day the price of securities traded on the New York Stock Exchange began to drop sharply. Within a month the value of these huge investments had shrunk by 40 per cent, a decline that triggered an economic disaster without precedent in our history.

When stock prices plummeted, a great many persons and a great many businesses went bankrupt. When banks could not recoup the money they had loaned, many also went bankrupt and their depositors lost their savings. As confidence in the economy withered, the amount spent on goods plunged, with the result that many companies shut down, many workers lost their jobs, and spending dropped still more. By 1932, 5000 banks had failed, factory production had been cut in half, and construction projects throughout the country virtually had ground to a halt. Over 13 million workers—one in four—were without jobs and millions more worked only part time. Wages that year came to but $31 billion, compared to $55 billion in 1929. Throughout the nation the mood was one of bewilderment, despair, and slowly mounting anger.

The unions also were hard hit. As the number of jobs continued to drop, so did union membership. By 1933 only 2.5 million workers, less than 5 per cent of the labor force, still belonged to unions. In the past the government would not have concerned itself about this. But now its officials were convinced that strong unions, with millions of unskilled and semiskilled workers, could spur the nation's economic recovery. Through bargaining with management they could raise wages and increase badly needed purchasing power. By providing a means to settle grievances, they also could provide a bulwark against revolution, which at that point seemed a distinct possibility.

In the end Congress passed the needed legislation. For the first time the Federal government guaranteed workers the right to organize and join unions. If at least 30 per cent in a company wanted a union, the government would poll all the workers affected. If a majority decided on a union, their employer had to bargain with it, whether or not he wanted to. Moreover, he was barred from forming company unions and from committing a long list of "unfair labor practices." For the first time in its long, frustrating history, labor had the help it needed (see chapter 11).

A GATHERING STORM

The result, as one observer put it, was a "frenzy of organizing." By 1934 hundreds of thousands of men and women had joined the Clothing Workers, the Mine Workers, and other unions, demanding that employers comply with the law and deal with their new locals. But many employers refused, convinced that the new regulations were unconstitutional. Instead they added labor spies and armed guards to their staffs, stockpiled guns, ammunition, and tear gas and, whenever workers struck for recognition, brought in strikebreakers. Violence erupted in San Francisco, Minneapolis, Toledo, and scores of other cities as workers insisted on their newly acquired rights and management fought back and frequently won. In this period, according to one Congressional report, American business spent $80 million a year fighting unionism.

Trouble also was brewing inside the labor movement. At stake was a strategy that would determine how successful labor would be in this explosive time. Despite the frenzy of organizing, the leaders of the craft unions that dominated the AFL urged caution. They could not forget cases when labor had expanded too rapidly and in the end had been weakened. To protect themselves they insisted that no new unions be formed, that all new recruits join their unions.

But a group of younger union presidents disagreed sharply. The massive organizing campaign that was under way had to be continued, they argued. Otherwise, an extraordinary opportunity would be lost. Organizing industrial unions also was essential, for only when all the workers in a company, skilled and unskilled, came together in a giant union could labor deal with a giant corporation.

In 1935 the AFL's leaders voted for caution and craft unions. The dissidents then formed the Committee for Industrial Organization, the CIO, and, under the leadership of fiery John L. Lewis of the Mine Workers, went their own way. Within three years the AFL would expel the unions headed by the dissidents, who then would form a rival federation, the Congress of Industrial Organizations, with Lewis as president.

"WHEN THE BOSS WON'T TALK, DON'T TAKE A WALK, SIT DOWN! SIT DOWN!"

When the AFL and the CIO began recruiting, and competing, in earnest in 1936 they had great difficulty keeping up with the demand for organizers. In fact, many workers organized local unions on their own, then tried to find a national union, often *any* national union, to take them. When their employers refused to recognize their new locals, they also turned to a form of passive resistance they called the "sit-down strike," in which they refused to leave their plant, shop, or office until their demands were met. One of the first sit-down strikes in this era actually occurred in 1934 when two baseball teams, each representing a rubber company, "sat down" until management provided a union man as an umpire. (In 1906 the Wobblies used this tactic in a "stay-in" strike at the General Electric plant in Schenectady, New York.) In 1936 a half million workers sat down—and with incredible success.[*]

The CIO concentrated in this period on organizing workers in the mass-production industries, particularly the rubber, automobile, and steel plants where their jobs as cogs in an endless assembly line had embittered and dehumanized them. Its major target was the General Motors Corporation,

---

[*] In the 1950s civil rights demonstrators borrowed this tactic to desegregate restaurants, swimming pools, and other public facilities in the South. A decade later university students used the sitdown—or the "sit-in," as they called it—to liberalize residential rules on their campuses and to change policies that permitted faculty members to conduct military research.

the world's largest company, where the United Auto Workers were fighting for recognition. In November 1936 the struggle approached its climax.

The GM plant in Atlanta was closed by a sit-down strike which then spread to factories in Kansas City, Cleveland, and Detroit. On December 30 the strike came to Flint, Michigan, the heart of the General Motors empire, when several hundred workers "sat down" in Fisher Body Plants 1 and 2. When a court ordered the workers to leave and they refused to do so, the Flint police tried to force them out. Hour after hour they pumped tear gas and buckshot into the plant, but the strikers refused to surrender. Instead they responded with a steady barrage of tools, pipes, bolts, and car door hinges. Meanwhile two hundred workers outside successfully charged the gates of the plant and joined them. Toward midnight the strikers turned a powerful fire hose on the police, drove them off, and held the plant. But twenty-four strikers and policemen had been injured.

To prevent further violence Michigan's governor, Frank Murphy, himself the grandson of an Irish revolutionary, ordered 1500 National Guardsmen to Flint. Meanwhile, union men had occupied two more plants, Chevrolet 4 and 9. When new efforts to end the strike broke down, the governor decided to remove the workers. But first he drove to Detroit, where John L. Lewis was staying, to plead with him to stop the strike and avoid further bloodshed. When Lewis refused, Murphy asked what he would do when the workers were ordered out.

"You want my answer, sir? I shall give it to you. Tomorrow morning I shall personally enter General Motors plant Chevrolet No. 4. I shall order the men to disregard your order. I shall then walk up to the largest window in the plant, open it, divest myself of my outer raiment, remove my shirt, and bare my bosom. Then, when you order your

Sit-down strikers at a General Motors plant in Flint, Michigan, in 1937.

troops to fire, mine will be the first breast those bullets will strike. And as my body falls from that window to the ground, you listen to the voice of your grandfather as he whispers in your ear, 'Frank, are you sure you are doing the right thing?' " *

The order to remove the workers never was issued. On February 11, under pressure from Governor Murphy and President Franklin D. Roosevelt, General Motors agreed to recognize the union. Led by a color guard bearing the American flag and by a band from the Detroit Musicians Union, the strikers marched from the buildings they had occupied in some cases for more than six weeks.

In March 1937 organizers for the Auto Workers moved on

---

* *New York Times*, June 12, 1969.

The "Memorial Day Massacre": Strikers against the Republic Steel Corporation march with their families toward the firm's South Chicago mill on Memorial Day, 1937. When police ordered them to disperse and they refused, a fatal clash resulted.

to the Chrysler Corporation and within two months won recognition there. In May the target was Ford, a company where discontent was so great that workers installed dead rats in the cars they built. But through legal maneuvers, intimidation, and improvements in working conditions, Ford was able to keep the union at bay until 1941, when the Federal government ordered a collective bargaining election. Of the 74,000 workers who voted, 72,000 asked for a union to represent them.

Meanwhile the CIO had formed the Steel Workers Organizing Committee, which later would become the United Steelworkers of America. With a $2 million fund, provided largely by the United Mine Workers, and a corps of 400 organizers the committee set to work. By spring they had organized 150,000 steel workers, and the giant of the industry, the United States Steel Corporation, agreed without a fight to recognize the union. Following its lead ninety other steel companies also signed contracts.

But several firms, known collectively as Little Steel, would not do so. Under the leadership of Republic Steel, terrorism and espionage became the order of the day in these companies. A writer for the *St. Louis Post-Dispatch* reported that workers who showed the slightest interest in unionism were fired and railroaded out of town. "An elaborate system of espionage permeated not only the plants but extended into the schools, churches, lodges, and even the homes," he wrote. "Nothing was too small to pass unnoticed. The most innocuous remark was apt to be carried to the boss, perhaps twisted in the telling. . . ." *

When Republic refused to recognize the union, 70,000 workers walked off the job in a bitter strike that reached its climax on a bright, sunny Memorial Day in 1937 in South

---

* Louis L. Snyder and Richard B. Morris, *A Treasury of Great Reporting* (New York: Simon & Schuster, 1949).

Chicago, where one of the Republic mills had remained open.

A thousand strikers and their families spent part of the day at a union rally about three blocks across a large field from the mill. Their objective, according to newspaper reports, was to march through the main gate and close the plant. Carrying banners, chanting "CIO! CIO!" the strikers, their wives, and their children walked across the field, armed, according to police, with bricks, clubs, chains, and firearms. Halfway to the gate, spread out in single file five blocks long, 160 policemen awaited them. Captain Thomas Kilroy stepped forward as they approached. "You can't get through here," he told them. "We must do our duty." *

According to police, the strikers persisted in pushing forward, hurling bricks and firing weapons as they advanced. Individual policemen then fired back in self-defense. Union accounts dispute this. They claim the strikers were peaceful, that the police fired without provocation at point blank range into the crowd, continued firing as the demonstrators and their families fled, then clubbed those who could not escape. Within but five minutes, ten strikers and strike sympathizers had been killed, and ninety other persons, including a number of policemen, had been seriously injured in what became known as the Memorial Day Massacre. Not until 1942, under mounting pressure from the Federal government, did Republic and the rest of Little Steel come to terms with the union.

Meanwhile the CIO had acquired a new president. John L. Lewis had resigned and Philip Murray had taken his place. Murray had headed the enormously successful Steel Workers Organizing Committee and earlier had worked with

---

* Ibid.

Lewis as a vice-president of the United Mine Workers. Lewis's resignation and the unionization of Little Steel were the last steps in a remarkable revolution. When the nation entered World War II in 1941, 9 million workers belonged to unions. By the time the war ended in 1945 their membership had climbed to almost 15 million, including many women who had been needed in defense plants. Labor at long last had become a national force.

A TIME TO CELEBRATE, A TIME TO WONDER

During the four years the war lasted the government tightly controlled labor–management relations. But when the war ended a new era began. For the first time in a large number of industries, workers and their employers negotiated wages, hours, and working conditions. But for many labor leaders and many managers this meant learning how to bargain. In a number of cases it also meant learning how to use power responsibly. As a result, the first years after the war were difficult ones for both sides. During 1945 and 1946 disputes over contract negotiations resulted in 10,000 strikes, a larger number than in any two-year period before or since. Unlike strikes in the past the vast majority were peaceful, but the public was deeply disturbed. Although either side can cause a strike, the great number that occurred seemed to support management's argument that labor had too much freedom, that the laws that created strong unions in the 1930s had gone too far, that the balance of power between the two had to be adjusted. In 1947, as a result, Congress imposed curbs on labor's freedom to organize new unions and to strike. But in the years ahead, the issue of labor's power would be raised again and again, at times with justification, but in other cases with none whatsoever (see chapter 11).

As the two sides adjusted to their new relationship, the number of strikes tapered off. But as labor struggled to establish stable, effective organizations, two serious problems arose. In a number of its unions, the AFL was faced with corruption and racketeering. In an effort to clean house it expelled one of its long-time affiliates, the International Longshoremen's Association. But not too many years later it also would have to deal with a half dozen others including the Teamsters, the nation's largest union (see chapter 9).

The CIO, on the other hand, was faced with a radically different problem: infiltration by Communists. Starting in the 1920s, after the Russian Revolution, an increasing number of Communists were hired by the unions, most of which traditionally were concerned not with a man's political beliefs but only with his seeming dedication to their cause. Some of those hired were part of an organized effort which originated in Moscow to take control of American unions, form a Communist labor party, and in this way influence the course of government. Their big chance came in 1935 when the CIO was formed and needed large numbers of organizers, publicity men, lawyers, and other specialists. Over the years many of the Communists employed rose to important positions in their unions. As their influence grew pressure to remove them also grew. After a major internal struggle, the CIO fired the Communists on its staff and in 1949 and 1950 expelled eleven Communist-dominated unions with almost 900,000 members (see chapters 18 and 19).

In 1952 William Green died after twenty-eight years as president of the AFL. Eleven days later so did Philip Murray, president of the CIO. Green was succeeded by George Meany, a blunt, forceful plumber from the Bronx who had

George Meany, left, president of the AFL, and Walter Reuther, president of the CIO, clasp hands in 1955 when their organizations became one.

TRADES-ALL CRAFTS-ALL COLORS-ALL CREEDS
—TOGETHER!
AMERICAN FEDERATION OF LABOR & CONGRESS OF INDUSTRIAL ORGANIZATIONS
AFL
CIO

risen to become the AFL's secretary–treasurer. Murray was replaced by Walter Reuther, the ultraliberal president of the United Auto Workers. With the changing of the guard came an opportunity for reconciliation. In 1955, after twenty years of disunity and rivalry, ninety-four national unions with 16 million members joined forces as the AFL–CIO, with George Meany as president.

Walter Reuther called the merger "a new beginning" and clearly it was. For many, labor's new strength held the promise of organizing the millions of workers still outside the labor movement, of dealing with a growing threat to jobs posed by automation, and of spearheading a massive drive to improve life in the United States for the underprivileged. But others wondered whether such a huge federation, inevitably remote from the workers, could revive the crusading spirit of the 1930s or whether it would become merely another bureaucracy concerned as much with its own survival as anything else. For the moment, however, such thoughts could be put aside. In but two decades, out of a hopeless shambles, had grown the largest labor federation in the world. A struggle that had begun 161 years earlier in the cordwainers' shops of Philadelphia had borne fruit. For labor it was a time to celebrate.

Part Two | THE MOVEMENT AND ITS MEMBERS

\With more than 20 million members, organized labor is today the largest mass movement in the United States. But it is not the centralized, single-minded monolith it may seem in the news reports. Instead it is a coalition of thousands of interlocking organizations bound together by a common desire for a larger share of the national abundance. The best known of these organizations is the AFL–CIO, but there also are international unions, local unions, state federations, district councils, local councils, and other groups, each with its own members, leaders, staff, objectives, programs, strategies, allies, and rivals.

4 | The Federation

The week before he left office, President Lyndon B. Johnson went to the headquarters of the AFL–CIO just across Lafayette Square from the White House to thank labor's leaders for the support they had given his program. "I know of no single group more responsible for the advances that have been made than the AFL–CIO," he told them. Not everyone regards the American Federation of Labor–Congress of Industrial Organizations as highly as did Mr. Johnson, but there are few in Washington or in other power centers who question its great influence on the course of events. With the public, however, there is a good deal of confusion as to just what the AFL–CIO is and what it does. It is not, as many believe, the largest and most powerful union in the United States. In fact, it is not a union at all. Instead, it is an association of international unions—a kind of union of unions—that operates at the heart of the labor movement. Some 130 international unions with 80 per cent of the nation's unionized workers are members.

The AFL–CIO's major task is strengthening the labor movement. It helps establish new unions and also assists existing unions in recruiting members. It aids in major strikes by organizing fund-raising efforts and boycotts. In schools it operates, including a year-round "labor college," it trains many of the leaders and specialists unions need. To make unionism more attractive to management it also promotes the sale of union-made goods. Over 3000 products carry labels indicating they were made by union workers and are of high quality.*

The federation also is deeply involved in national affairs. Since many of labor's goals can be achieved only through legislation, it supports politicians who are sympathetic to its viewpoint and lobbies vigorously and often successfully in the Congress for a wide range of programs (see chapter 18). It also is concerned with foreign affairs, particularly with stopping the spread of Communism abroad. Its major efforts involve the newly developing countries of Latin America, Africa, and Asia. With grants from the State Department and with its own funds, it works to develop "free, democratic" trade unions in these areas as a bulwark against Communism (see chapter 19).

---

* A union-made sport jacket will have such a label in the inside breast pocket. With a skirt it may be sewn into the waistband or be attached under the manufacturer's label.

The AFL–CIO operates through a nationwide network of organizations, which is depicted in the chart on page 66. There are labor federations in each of the fifty states and local federations, or central labor councils, in each of 900 cities and counties. In addition, six AFL–CIO departments concerned with unions in particular industries have 900 offices of their own. About $12 million a year is needed to operate the federation. Its funds come from the international unions which contribute ten cents a month per member. This may not seem like much but for the largest unions it represents an annual contribution of over a million dollars. The state and local federations are supported through similar levies paid by the local unions.

In theory the AFL–CIO is run by its member unions. Every other year almost 1000 union delegates meet to review labor's problems and determine what to do about them. In practice, it is the officers they elect who make the final decisions. These include a full-time president, a full-time secretary–treasurer, and thirty-three vice-presidents, each the head of a national union. Together they make up an executive council, a kind of council of tribal chieftains, which runs the federation. They are shown at one of their meetings in the photograph at the beginning of this chapter.

There are seventy international unions with over 5 million members that do not belong to the AFL–CIO. They include the nation's two largest unions, the Teamsters and the United Auto Workers, and one of its oldest, the venerated United Mine Workers, from whose ranks have come three presidents of labor federations: John L. Lewis and Philip Murray of the CIO and William Green of the AFL. Some unions remain outside the federation because their leaders see no advantage in joining. But there also are other reasons. A number of unions, including the Teamsters, once were part

STRUCTURE OF THE LABOR
MOVEMENT IN THE UNITED STATES

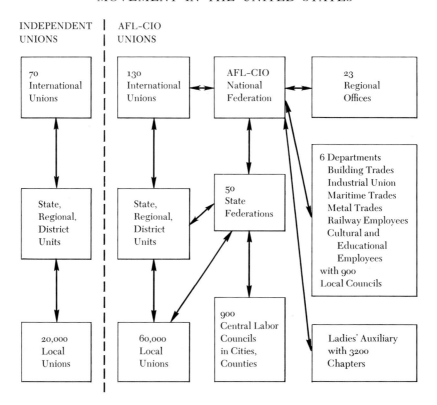

INDEPENDENT
UNIONS

AFL–CIO
UNIONS

70
International
Unions

130
International
Unions

AFL–CIO
National
Federation

23
Regional
Offices

State,
Regional,
District
Units

State,
Regional,
District
Units

50
State
Federations

6 Departments
  Building Trades
  Industrial Union
  Maritime Trades
  Metal Trades
  Railway Employees
  Cultural and
    Educational
    Employees
with 900
Local Councils

20,000
Local
Unions

60,000
Local
Unions

900
Central Labor
Councils
in Cities,
Counties

Ladies' Auxiliary
with 3200
Chapters

of the federation or one of its predecessors and were expelled for corruption. Others were cast out when they came under the domination of Communism (see chapters 3 and 9). The United Electrical Workers of America was one of these. However, it purged itself of Communist influences and today has 160,000 members. Others have withdrawn over policy differences. The Auto Workers, for example, withdrew when its leaders decided that the federation was not working hard enough to expand unionism.

But what is remarkable about the labor movement are not the differences, but the degree of unity that persists. In part this is rooted in tradition. The movement is the single American institution that speaks for the working man. But there is a more compelling reason. The unions need one another. Together they are stronger than they are alone. Labor's leaders know this only too well.

*IAM head-
quarters*

5 | IAM,
AFSCME, UFWOC

An international union is a nation unto itself. Each has a unique history, its own government, its own way of doing things. In each, moreover, the members share needs and problems that do not exist in other unions.

The International Association of Machinists (IAM) was organized at a secret meeting in a locomotive pit in Atlanta in 1888. Its founding fathers were nineteen dissatisfied railroad machinists, whose job it was to create metal parts. But they also were "boomers," a restless breed that moved from freight yard to freight yard and job to job. In their travels they planted the seeds of unionism far and wide, with results they might find hard to believe.

Their union's symbol still is a high-precision gear, but the union itself now represents a million workers in 15,000 companies. In addition to railroad machinists, they include mechanics, flight engineers, and passenger agents for the airline industry, production workers in the aerospace industry, and miners, taxi drivers, cafeteria workers, and men and women in a score of other occupations clustered in 2000 local unions.

The union's headquarters is a well-carpeted, ten-story building in Washington, D.C. Its staff of three hundred includes economists, wage analysts, statisticians, mathematicians, programmers who operate the union's computers, lawyers, organizers, publicity experts, political experts, librarians, journalists who produce a weekly newspaper, a speech writer, and a specialist who deals with unions abroad (see Careers in Labor Relations).

The Machinists also have four hundred offices throughout the country from which a thousand union representatives help local unions with their problems. Although the union continues to organize new locals, its major job today is providing services. In exchange for their monthly dues, it negotiates contracts for members, handles their complaints about employers, lobbies in their behalf, and helps in other ways. For all its operations it spends about $30 million a year, as much as a medium-sized corporation. In fact, in many respects it resembles just that.

The American Federation of State, County, and Municipal Employees (AFSCME) had 400,000 members when this was written. As you read this its membership undoubtedly is far larger, for AFSCME was the fastest growing union in the country. And others that organized government workers were not far behind.

For most of these unions growth and power were a new experience. Up to the 1950s they had been small, weak organizations.* One reason for this was government policy. When Congress established the right to bargain through unions, it excluded government workers on the ground that a government cannot share its power and therefore cannot bargain. But economics also stood in the way. A government job provided a good wage and generous benefits. As government workers saw it, there was no need to join a union. When wages began to lag, however, pressure for the right to bargain mounted and union membership began to grow.

Late in the 1950s, first Philadelphia, then New York agreed to bargain with the unions its employees had formed. In 1961 New York's teachers won this right from the city's Board of Education. The following year Federal employees were given the right to bargain and when a number of state and local governments followed suit, the rush was on. It was reminiscent of the 1930s when factory workers first were unionized. In a single decade a million government workers joined unions. Some joined AFSCME, but others joined the American Federation of Government Employees, the International Association of Fire Fighters, the American Federation of Teachers, the National Education Association, and a half dozen other rapidly expanding organizations. In some states public employees still do not have the right to bargain, but more and more join unions and more and more win this

------

* Two exceptions were the Letter Carriers and the Postal Clerks, which had large memberships and great influence in Congress where the question of raises for Federal employees was decided.

1200 striking sanitation workers in Memphis march on City Hall to dramatize their demands for job improvements.

right. When this was written over 3 million workers in government were union members (see chapters 15 and 16).

AFSCME's members are a curious mixture. Many are psychiatrists, architects, welfare workers, librarians, and ministers. But many are garbage collectors, floor moppers, maids, and other poorly educated people who often are not paid enough to make ends meet.

Their struggles with employers invariably are concerned with fair treatment as well as fair pay and often are as much a civil rights matter as they are a union cause. AFSCME is strongest in northern cities—in New York it has over 90,000 members—but some of its most important battles have taken place in the South, including this encounter in 1968 in Memphis:

Some 1300 garbage collectors and sewer cleaners were involved. Most were members of AFSCME Local 1733, a newly-formed union. Most were also black, poor, and increasingly angry. They had demanded recognition for their union, a higher wage than the $1.60 an hour they were being

paid, and an end to discrimination on the job, but city officials ignored them. Their anger boiled over on a gloomy spring day when a heavy rain made it impossible to clean the sewers. When twenty-two black workers were sent home, but white workers were kept on, they struck and all garbage pickups in Memphis stopped. The mayor announced he would consider their grievances only when they returned to work, but under no circumstances would he deal with their union.

The result was a major racial confrontation. The city's 300,000 whites generally sided with the mayor. Its 200,000 blacks rallied to support the strikers. To increase pressure on the city the union organized mass meetings and protest marches. A steady stream of labor officials and civil rights leaders came to Memphis to lend their support. One was Martin Luther King, Jr., who was to have led a protest march but was shot to death the night before. Union sympathizers from across the country hurried to Memphis to march in his place. Arms linked, more than 40,000 marched through the city that day singing "We Shall Overcome."

But the mayor of Memphis would not yield and the union would not back down, and the potential for violence grew. Only after several telephone calls from the White House did the mayor agree to meet most of the union's demands. In the months that followed a flood of new members joined AFSCME in places like Jacksonville, Florida, Columbus, Georgia, and Pascadula, Mississippi. Most were black men who collected garbage and cleaned sewers.

Delano is a town of about 15,000 people some 130 miles northeast of Los Angeles. It is a trading center in the heart of California's lush San Joaquin Valley, one of the nation's major sources of fruit and vegetables. It also is headquarters for the United Farm Workers Organizing Committee

(UFWOC), whose goal it is to organize a national union of farm workers.

The major crop in the area is grapes. Some of the men and women who harvest them live in Delano. But many others are migratory workers. Each year they begin their labors far to the south near San Diego and slowly work their way north. Over the years Chinese, Japanese, Filipinos, and Mexicans all have followed this route. During the Great Depression they were joined by "Okies" and "Arkies," the refugees from the Great Plains of whom John Steinbeck wrote in *The Grapes of Wrath*. Today there are over 300,000 farm workers in California, most of whom are Mexican–Americans. Like farm workers everywhere they do not have an easy time. Usually they work only seven or eight months a year, but in this period they put in twelve hours a day at backbreaking labor for low wages. Many also live under the most unpleasant conditions, often in shacks without windows, running water, or electricity. Over the years they have made sporadic attempts to improve their lot by forming unions, but the growers were not required by law to deal with them and usually their efforts lost them their jobs.

It was not until 1962 that change became a possibility. The person responsible was a community organizer named Cesar Chavez, who as a boy had followed the harvest with his family. So often did they move, he attended thirty-one elementary schools. Chavez had been working in the Mexican–American ghetto in San Jose helping families there develop the leaders and organizations they needed to improve their lives. After several years at this, he decided to try these methods with the grape pickers. If he could help them to develop leaders of their own and increase their self-confidence, there might be a chance, he felt, to build a successful union. Two other organizers agreed to join him. One was Dolores Huerta, a former schoolteacher. The other was

Cesar Chavez,
founder of the
Farm Workers union.

Fred Ross, who had come to California thirty years before as an Okie. Chavez, his wife, and their eight children moved to Delano, and he set to work.

He called his organization the National Farm Workers Association (NFWA). As a symbol he selected the thunderbird, the mythical source of thunder and lightning, which Mexicans had used to symbolize earlier struggles. The dues would be $3.50 a month, when a family could pay. In return, NFWA eventually would provide life insurance, a credit union through which a member could borrow money, a service center where he could bring his personal problems, a health clinic, a cooperative store, and a newspaper. It also would lobby to change the state's laws so that farm workers, like other workers, would have unemployment insurance, workmen's compensation in case of injury, and the right to bargain through a union.

In the first year Chavez, Ross, and Mrs. Huerta signed up 300 members. "I went to 87 labor camps," Chavez recalled, "and in each I'd find a few people who were committed to doing something. Something had happened in their lives and they were ready. . . ." Within three years they had recruited 2000 members up and down the valley and finally could make good on some of their promises. But as yet they had done nothing to raise wages. That would require a strike and Chavez did not think the organization was strong enough. However, events soon would force his hand.

Far to the south in the Coachella Valley, the AFL–CIO had also organized a group of farm workers. Early in 1965 they demanded a pay increase and much to their surprise it was granted. By late summer they had worked their way north to Delano to help bring in the grape harvest. When they arrived, they made the same demands they had made earlier, but this time they were turned down, and they struck. A week later members of NFWA voted to join them.

Of course, striking was one thing. Forcing the growers to capitulate was another. To do so they would have to convince the workers who had replaced them to join in the strike. But with thirty-four vineyards to cover, the task was formidable. The two groups organized roving picket lines that traveled from vineyard to vineyard in a caravan of broken-down cars. When they spotted men and women in the fields, they stopped their cars, lined up at the edge of the road, and through a bullhorn urged them to leave their jobs, shouting "Huelga! Huelga!—Strike! Strike!" The growers retaliated by spraying them with insecticide and shooting at their picket signs. To keep the cars running, NFWA set up a garage in Delano. To help the strikers make ends meet, it gave them meals in a community kitchen and paid their rent and utility bills.

The strike caught the imagination of unionists, civil rights

*Clustered at the edge of a vineyard, striking
grape pickers urge those still on the job to join them.*

leaders, churchmen, students, and ordinary citizens. Some responded with money. Others gave food. Each day, for example, a bakery in Los Angeles sent 100 loaves of bread and each week a union in San Francisco sent 1200 eggs. In addition, many college students gave their time, working as pickets or drivers or helpers in the strike office.

When it became clear, however, that the grape harvest could not be stopped, the two groups changed their strategy. They would concentrate on one grower with a well-known product, picket his operation as before, but rely on a boycott to force him to the bargaining table. Their first target was a vineyard operated by Schenley Distillers, which used its grapes to produce wine it then marketed throughout the country. Members of the Retail Clerks union and of CORE,

*A singular victory:
union recognition and
union label grapes.*

the civil rights group, picketed hundreds of Schenley outlets from coast to coast. When sales dropped sharply Schenley quickly recognized the two unions and raised wages, and a dozen other wine producers followed its lead. Encouraged by this victory, the two pooled their members and resources in a single organization, the United Farm Workers Organizing Committee, with Chavez as director.

The new union next turned to growers of table grapes. Guimarra Vineyards, one of the world's largest producers, was the target. A boycott again would be the major weapon, but since it was impossible to single out Guimarra's grapes, all California grapes would be boycotted. Fifty farm workers led by Mrs. Huerta drove east in a school bus to organize support for the effort. In New York, Boston, Chicago, and other cities, they told their story to thousands of organizations and enlisted tens of thousands of volunteers who picketed food stores where grapes were sold, urged government

officials not to buy grapes for use in schools and hospitals, wrote letters to growers demanding that they recognize the union, and distributed an unending stream of literature.

The growers fought back with an advertising campaign. In addition, a number of right-wing organizations came to their aid. The American Farm Bureau organized an "Eat Grapes" campaign which won the support of California governor Ronald Reagan and Richard Nixon, who then was running for President. The National Right to Work Committee, an antiunion group, sponsored a nationwide speaking tour for farm workers who were critical of Cesar Chavez. And the John Birch Society attacked the boycott as a "Communist plot."

But the boycott worked. Sales of grapes dropped by more than half. After four years Guimarra recognized the union and in the months that followed other growers also did. Yet only a beginning had been made. There still were huge numbers of farm workers who toiled for pennies and lived in squalor. This was the case not only in California, but in New Mexico, Arizona, Texas, Wisconsin, Florida, New York, and New Jersey. Whether they could be organized into a national union, no one knew. That the effort would be made, however, seemed clear.

6 | The Internationals

The men who run the international unions are political men who hold offices by virtue of the support they have managed to develop over the years. Often this is based on their ability and personality, but as in any political job, the favors a man does and the jobs he dispenses also are factors. In a few cases strong-arm tactics and intimidation also play a role. Almost all these leaders are self-made men who helped organize their unions or started as officials of local unions and diligently worked their way to the top. Leonard Woodcock, president of the United Auto Workers, started in a machine shop. Paul Hall, president of the Seafarers Union, was a wiper aboard a merchant ship. Matthew Guinan, president of the Transport Workers Union, was a motorman in New York's subway. Joseph Byrne, president of the Communications Workers, was an errand boy.

Unlike their counterparts in management, most union officers also are self-educated men who have acquired on their own a working knowledge of economics, business practices, politics, and other subjects basic to their jobs. Only in recent years, in fact, have college-educated labor leaders begun to appear. Women in high positions also are few and far between, even in unions where women make up most of the membership (see chapter 8).

A union's top officials usually include a president and a secretary–treasurer, who is second in command. In large unions there also is a retinue of vice-presidents. All are excellent jobs which provide power, prestige, and an ample salary. According to one study, the presidents of the twenty largest unions are paid, on the average, over $40,000 a year. A half dozen earn over $50,000. One, the president of the Teamsters, receives $100,000. He also has use of an elaborate executive suite, which includes a heavily carpeted, walnut-paneled office, with a built-in television receiver, high fidelity system, and bar, plus a steam room, a gymnasium, and a movie theater. However, most union officials make do with far less.

Once a man is elected to high office, he usually remains until he decides to retire, with the result that a great many union leaders are older men. Although they must stand for re-election periodically, in many unions the procedure is little more than a formality. Usually such elections take place at a union convention where delegates from the local unions make the decision. The re-election of Jerry Wurf as president of the State, County, and Municipal Employees was typical.

VICE-PRESIDENT BLATZ: . . . I could go on and on, but, brothers and sisters, I put it before you. The ship of our union has been repaired, and put in shape. The decks have been cleared. The course has been charted. The shakedown cruise is over. The weather is fair. We are ready for our voyage to greatness. (Applause) There are two things for us to do and this Convention must do them. We must supply the fuel. We must pick the Captain . . . . At this time I need not nominate—the record nominates the only possible, logical choice for that task—your President and mine, Jerry Wurf! (Standing ovation)

VICE-PRESIDENT CRIPPEN: Will the President accept?

PRESIDENT WURF: Ask for further nominations. (Laughter and applause)

VICE-PRESIDENT CRIPPEN: I wanted to see if he would run. Are there further nominations?

DELEGATE FROM THE FLOOR: I move the nominations be closed.

VICE-PRESIDENT CRIPPIN: No. Are there further nominations? (No response) Are there further nominations? (No response) . . . I now declare the President of this Organization for the ensuing two years to be Jerry Wurf! (Standing ovation) *

There are unions, however, in which a vigorous fight for high office is a tradition. One such organization is the United Steelworkers whose million members select their officers through a secret ballot. Another is the International Typographical Union, which for many years has had a two-party

---

* Proceedings of the 16th International Convention, AFSCME, 1966.

system. Of course, a power struggle may develop no matter what the tradition. Jerry Wurf himself came to office in a heated election which saw a group of younger officials overthrow the founder of the union who, in their view, was no longer producing results. But it is extremely difficult to successfully challenge a union president. He has a staff that does his bidding. He controls the union newspaper or magazine. He has the funds and the freedom to visit local unions throughout the country. And often he is free to fire anyone on his staff who opposes him.

If a serious challenge does arise, the contest is likely to be heated. "You are lower than scum!" Joseph Curran, president of the National Maritime Union, shouted when his challengers appeared at the union convention. "Rip this cancer out of your bowels!" David MacDonald, then president of the Steelworkers, roared to convention delegates when he was challenged. But far more than words may be involved. If a challenger loses, and he is a member of the union's staff, he is likely to lose his job and other staff members who supported him are likely to lose theirs. Of course, if he wins, those who opposed him may be purged.

BOYLE AND YABLONSKI

One of the most dramatic struggles for control of a union in modern times took place in 1969. The union was the United Mine Workers of America which the famed John L. Lewis had ruled for forty years without challenge. But his successor, a former Montana coal miner named Tony Boyle, did not have such good fortune. When he announced he would run for a second five-year term, a union vice-president named Joseph A. Yablonski said he would oppose him.

Yablonski saw much to criticize in Boyle. He claimed he

was a "corrupt dictator" who used union funds as if they were his own, kept relatives on the union payroll at fat salaries, and maintained an unhealthy alliance with operators of the coal mines where the members worked. He said that despite inflation, retired miners had not had their pensions improved in years, yet the union's top officers secretly had voted themselves pensions at full salary, which in Boyle's case was $50,000 a year. He said that the union, in collusion with mine owners, was doing nothing to improve safety and health in the mines even though men were being killed and injured and others were being disabled by "black lung" disease.

Boyle denied none of this. Instead he campaigned vigorously for re-election, visiting union hall after union hall, vowing to make the union "a democratic servant of the members." Under Yablonski's goading, he joined the effort to improve safety and health in the mines. He also saw to it that pensions were increased. Yablonski, meanwhile, filed complaint after complaint with the Federal government, charging that Boyle was using union funds and union staff members in his campaign. At one point he sued the union to force its weekly newspaper, the *UMW Journal,* to report that he was running against Boyle. In a thirty-four-page issue, for example, the *Journal* carried thirty-eight different pictures of Boyle, but not a word about Yablonski. Only when he won his suit did the paper acknowledge that he was a candidate. Violence also played a role. Toward the end of the campaign an unknown assailant knocked Yablonski unconscious with a karate blow to the neck.

When the votes were counted, the union reported 81,056 for Boyle and 45,872 for Yablonski. Yablonski called the election "dishonest," demanded a government investigation, and declared he would continue to fight for reform, using his of-

Joseph Yablonski, top, and Tony Boyle, bottom, as they campaigned for the presidency of the United Mine Workers.

fice of vice-president as a base of operations. (Since he was an elected official, he could not be fired.) Three weeks after the election, responding to pressures he had helped mobilize, the Congress passed a law which required safer, more healthful conditions in the mines. That night or the following one, no one was sure, Yablonski and his wife and daughter were murdered at their home in Clarksville, Pennsylvania, near Pittsburgh. Twenty thousand miners walked off their jobs in rage. Union officials denied knowledge of the crime and posted a $50,000 reward for those responsible. Meanwhile, the United States Department of Labor launched an investigation of the election and a Senate committee began an investigation of the union.

BREAD, BUTTER, AND SOLIDARITY

Not all unions have the same goals or the same programs. A number are economic pressure groups whose only objective is to raise wages and protect their members on the job. They restrict their activities to negotiating contracts, lobbying for favorable legislation, and organizing new locals (see chapters 13 to 18). The Teamsters are in this category and so are many craft unions. Within the labor movement they are known as "business unions" or "bread and butter unions," since winning more bread and more butter is their primary concern. However, there also are unions with a broader focus. They are concerned not only with problems on the job, but with programs to improve their members' lives. The garment unions first used this approach early in this century to meet the needs of the impoverished Jewish and Italian immigrants who were their members. Today a sizable number of unions follows their lead.

Some unions operate ambitious educational programs. Through full-time schools or special courses, they train members to qualify for better jobs and help others earn high school diplomas they failed to obtain earlier. Through courses in union halls and summer programs on university campuses, which 15,000 local leaders attend each year, they teach the techniques of bargaining, settling disputes, and running a strike. They also distribute vast quantities of books, pamphlets, records, films, and other materials on unionism and social issues through which they hope to build loyalty to the labor movement.

Some unions also work vigorously to protect the health of their members, going well beyond the insurance protection most negotiate with employers. They arrange time off with pay for physical examinations, sell prescriptions at low cost, and operate clinics where members receive free help with their health problems. The Ladies' Garment Workers' Union has nineteen such clinics, including six mobile units in areas where its members are scattered. A growing number of unions also sponsor community health centers that concentrate on preventing disease and serve the public as well as their members. The Community Health Association of Detroit, whose principal sponsor is the United Auto Workers, is one such unit. For a small monthly fee, a family obtains any services it needs, from a physical examination to major surgery.

Some unions also provide housing for their members. At one extreme is the National Maritime Union, which rents rooms at reasonable rates to merchant seamen. At the other end are unions led by the Amalgamated Clothing Workers, which build cooperative apartment houses for unionists and others with moderate incomes through a foundation they operate. The largest of these projects is Co-op City in New York, a $300 million development with apartments for 55,000

TOP: *A school at Piney Point, Maryland, where
the Seafarers International Union trains merchant seamen.*
BOTTOM: *Co-op City, a housing project in New York,
sponsored by the Amalgamated Clothing Workers and other unions.*

persons. The group borrows the construction costs through its foundation, then repays the loans with the monthly payments the tenants make. When a tenant's payments reach a certain amount, moreover, the apartment is his.

International unions also have other activities that ordinarily are not associated with the labor movement. The Seafarers Union operates nonprofit cafeterias and taverns in various ports for its members. The Carpenters maintain a retirement home in Florida. The United Transportation Union sells its members low-cost insurance. The Amalgamated Clothing Workers runs a bank in New York which dates to the days when banks would not lend clothing workers money because their wages were too low. In addition, the American Federation of Teachers underwrites research on educational issues, the Air Line Pilots Associations sponsor an annual safety forum, and the Musicians union helps young people become string musicians.

The largest international unions spend millions of dollars a year on their activities. But even the smallest may have a budget of $100,000 or more. To meet their expenses all rely on the monthly dues their members pay. These range from about six dollars for a factory worker to over fifty dollars for members of some professional organizations. Through a system called the "checkoff," a member's employer withholds the money from his pay, then turns it over to his local union, which shares it with the international. A few unions also have other sources of income. The United Mine Workers operates the third largest bank in the nation's capital, the National Bank of Washington. The Communications Workers and other unions with buildings of their own rent office space. The Major League Baseball Players Association sells companies the right to refer to its members on their products and in their advertising. In a recent year businessmen paid over $300,000 for this privilege. But in this case the union's members shared the income.

Every few years officials from local unions all over the country convene to review the state of their international union. In the larger organizations over a thousand delegates participate. They listen to countless speeches, discuss union business at great length, pass scores of resolutions on union and national matters, and elect officers to serve until the next convention. But of equal importance, they come together as a union. They sing the old union songs, call one another "brother" or "sister," as is traditional, and reaffirm their solidarity, without which their union is nothing.

A delegate from a local union speaks his mind at a convention of the United Automobile Workers.

7 | The Locals

Local 781, United Brotherhood of Carpenters and Joiners of America, operates out of a small room behind Moore's Mower Shop in Princeton, New Jersey. Its 180 members include carpenters, apprentices who are learning carpentry at union expense, and supervisors who oversee work crews on construction jobs.

Typically a carpenter will work on a dozen or more projects in the course of a year, shifting from one to the next as he is needed. To make certain he has work, his union operates a hiring hall to which unionized builders turn when they need help. If such a builder hires nonunion carpenters, the local construction unions will boycott his project until the men are fired. The hiring hall is run by the local's business agent, who is its only full-time employee. He also deals with complaints members have about their jobs and represents the union in bargaining.

Like many local unions in the construction industry, Local 781 traditionally has had only white members. Its business agent says that in recent years the union has made strenuous efforts to attract black and Puerto Rican apprentices but that few apply and of those accepted none remain. However, some blacks insist discrimination is at work (see chapter 8).

With a monopoly of carpenters in its area, Local 781 is more powerful than any of the builders with whom it deals. In fact, it easily could destroy a builder's business by withholding its labor. To balance this power, the builders have formed an association, a kind of union of businessmen, through which they deal with the union as one on wage rates, benefits, and other matters. Of course, in many respects the union itself resembles a business, one whose product is the labor of its members.

Local 80A of the Amalgamated Meat Cutters and Butcher Workmen of North America has its headquarters in the heart of the black ghetto in Camden, New Jersey, in a gloomy, cavernous building that once was a post office. It represents 3000 workers in the Campbell Soup Company's plant just a few blocks away, and the odor of simmering soup is strong. Its members are the cooks who make the soup, the women who prepare the ingredients, and the men who form the cans, print the labels, and pack the cartons.

Every two years they elect three officers to run the union. Since these are full-time jobs, the local pays them a salary equal to what they would have made in the plant. In addition, they select about 100 men and women to serve part time as shop stewards. Their job is to represent the union inside the plant. This involves helping members with complaints they have and seeing to it that management lives up to its contract with the union. The company gives them time off to handle these duties and the union makes up the wages they lose.

The president of the local is a former soup cook. When I talked with him the union had just come off a four-and-a-half-week strike, through which it had won a new contract with higher wages and better benefits. But this local is concerned with more than bread and butter. If a member acquires more debts than he can handle, the union contacts the stores involved and tries to work out an easier payment schedule. If he gets in trouble with the law, the union sends him to a good lawyer. If he has personal problems at home, one of the officers is available for help. "My door is always open," the president told me. When I left, the row of chairs outside his office was filled.

The United Federation of Teachers is one of the largest and most powerful local unions in the United States. (Its other official designation is Local 2, American Federation of Teachers.) It represents more than 55,000 teachers, guidance counselors, librarians, and other workers in New York City's nine hundred public schools. Its full-time staff of sixty, most of whom are former teachers, is larger than that of many international unions. This also is true of its budget, which exceeds $1 million a year, and of its headquarters in an office building it owns a few blocks from Union Square.

Since the day in 1961 when the union became bargaining agent for New York's teachers, it has been a controversial force in the life of the city. With a million school children involved, it could not be otherwise. A highly militant organization, it has not hesitated to make any demands it regards as important to its members' well-being. Nor has it hesitated to back up these demands with a strike, even though strikes by public employees are illegal in New York State. Four times in its first seven years its members walked off the job when the Board of Education refused to go along with what the union wanted. In one strike the schools remained closed for two months.

These strikes had a curious result. On one hand, the union was punished for striking in defiance of the law. Twice it was fined at the rate of $10,000 a day and twice its president, Albert Shanker, a former mathematics teacher, was jailed. When confronted with the need to reopen its schools, however, the Board granted much of what the union sought. Although the Board had indicated it did not have the funds, pay was increased and benefits were expanded. In addition, the size of classes was reduced and for the first time teachers were given a voice in developing educational policies. "The city has convinced us," Shanker said, "that striking brings us gains we . . . cannot get in any other way."

The union's success spurred the organization of teacher unions throughout the country. But its strikes also underscored important questions about the use of union power, the responsibility of government to bargain in good faith, and the need for effective machinery to provide an alternative to strikes against the government.

THE SEEDBED

The 80,000 local unions in this country are where the basic work of unionism is done. Frequently they negotiate contracts with management that set wages, hours, and working conditions. They see to it that the terms of these contracts are enforced. They make certain that workers with complaints about their jobs get a fair hearing. They have responsibility for recruiting new members and turning them into loyal unionists. In addition, they bear the burden of strikes. It is the local union, scholars say, that is the "seedbed" of American unionism. It is where unionism takes root, where it grows or withers.

In legal terms every local union is a "bargaining agent" and the workers it represents are a "bargaining unit." Otherwise, the 80,000 locals differ in as many ways as internationals do. They may represent all the workers in a factory, a school, or a store or they may include only workers in certain jobs. They may be huge organizations that hold their meetings every month in a vast auditorium. Or they may have but a handful of members who are a closely knit brotherhood. They may be wealthy or they may be poor. They may be militant and powerful or they may be weak. They may have excellent relationships with management or there may be unbending hostility on both sides.

A number of locals are independent organizations with no outside ties. But the vast majority are part of an international union. The Bakery Workers Union, for example, consists of 300 separate locals. Like most internationals, it provides them with various services, reviews and approves the contracts they negotiate, and gives or withholds permission to strike. Moreover, each is assigned an international representative who participates in negotiations and helps in other ways. Most local unions also belong to two other organizations, a central labor council which coordinates all union activities in a city or county and a state labor federation which lobbies in the state legislature for laws that benefit unions and their members.

How strong a union is depends in part on these relation-ships. But it depends even more on a complicated legal rela-tionship. To serve as bargaining agent for the workers in a plant or an office, a union's members must include at least half the workers involved. However, it must represent *everyone* in the bargaining unit, even if they are not mem-bers of the union. As a result, a local union may negotiate contracts and handle grievances for 5000 workers, yet ac-tually only have a bare majority of dues-paying members. Those who are not members receive the union's services free. Moreover, they need not support the union in its activi-ties, which means it cannot always present a united front ei-ther in bargaining or striking.

To protect itself against these possibilities, a local union tries to negotiate a "union security" agreement which re-quires that all workers it represents become union members if they want to keep their jobs. But whether it can win such an arrangement depends on its bargaining power with man-agement. In the 1930s the strongest unions won a "closed shop" under which an employer agreed to hire only union members, but Congress declared this practice illegal in 1947 when it passed the Taft–Hartley Act (see chapter 11). Today the strongest unions win a "union shop," under which a worker must join within a month or two if he wishes to keep his job, but now management may choose those workers it wishes to hire.

Weaker unions may negotiate an "agency shop," under which a worker who does not wish to join pays a fee for the services he receives. Or they may obtain another arrange-ment under which union membership is voluntary, but those who join must remain members for a specified period.

There also are many local unions which operate in an "open shop," where workers need not join or pay a fee even though a union works in their behalf. In some cases a union

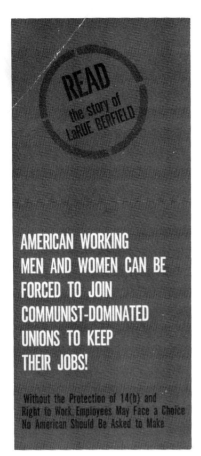

READ the story of LaRUE BENFIELD

AMERICAN WORKING MEN AND WOMEN CAN BE FORCED TO JOIN COMMUNIST-DOMINATED UNIONS TO KEEP THEIR JOBS!

Without the Protection of 14(b) and Right to Work, Employees May Face a Choice No American Should Be Asked to Make

"SO-CALLED 'RIGHT-TO-WORK' WILL ROB US OF OUR CIVIL RIGHTS AND JOB RIGHTS"

SAYS: REV. MARTIN LUTHER KING, JR.—HAILED AS "MAN-OF-THE-YEAR"

VOTE **NO** ON STATE QUESTION **409**

...so-called "RIGHT-TO-WORK"

LEFT: *A pamphlet urging state laws to ban the union shop.*
RIGHT: *A flyer opposing passage of such a law in Oklahoma.*

is not strong enough to win a better arrangement, but frequently it is the law that stands in the way. In many states so-called right-to-work laws ban union security agreements on the ground that a worker should have the freedom to join a union or not as he sees fit, even though the union must bargain for him. But union officials argue that if they must represent everyone, then everyone should join. They contend that the purpose of right-to-work laws is to weaken unions and thereby reduce, not increase, a worker's freedom. The battle over union security has been joined in forty states, with businessmen, farm leaders, and other conservative forces on one side and labor unions and liberal groups on the other.*

Ironically, there also are many workers who want to join a union, but are unable to do so. When they try to form a new local they may be thwarted by the opposition of their employer or by the refusal of an international union to help because the task seems too difficult or because the return in dues would not be great enough. If they are black, Puerto Rican, or Mexican—American, they frequently have another problem. Some of the skilled craft unions in the building trades will not admit them as members. The AFL–CIO has vowed to eliminate this discrimination, but it persists (see chapters 8 and 13).

A QUEST FOR POWER

Like all governments, those that run the local unions consist of an executive (the officers), a legislature (the members), and a judiciary (the officers or the members). The typical local is administered by part-time volunteers who serve in a dozen different positions, from president and treasurer to shop steward and sergeant at arms. Only the craft unions and the larger locals, like the teachers' union in New York and the workers in the soup kitchen in Camden, New Jersey, have officers who work full time and are paid salaries.

But even for an officer who does not receive pay, there are compensations, particularly if his regular job is a monotonous dead end. Thus, he may spend as much as half the

---

* The following states had right-to-work laws in 1971: Alabama, Arizona, Arkansas, Florida, Georgia, Iowa, Kansas, Mississippi, Nebraska, Nevada, North Carolina, North Dakota, South Carolina, South Dakota, Tennessee, Texas, Utah, Virginia, Wyoming.

week away from his regular job, for which his union or employer pays him. Usually he also has an expense account and is exempt from paying union dues. Moreover, he is a man of consequence in his union and in his community. He deals with his employer as an equal. His support may be sought by civic leaders and political figures. His ideas may be reported in the local newspaper. He also may attend leadership schools and conventions his international union sponsors and, if he is a good officer, eventually he may be offered a job as an international representative. If he is defeated in a bid for re-election, therefore, it may be a decided wrench to return to the more ordinary life he led earlier.

In some unions there is a hard-fought contest for office as members form factions with their own candidates. Often such races are popularity contests, but at times serious issues emerge, such as whether the current officers have been forceful enough in dealing with management. As black unionists have grown in number, some have organized groups of their own through which they hope to win control of their unions. In some cases a union's officers are so deeply entrenched they are elected again and again with little opposition. Even if they ignore the rights of the members or are dishonest, as a small number are, it is difficult to remove them. As long as they negotiate good contracts, the members often are willing to overlook such behavior. From time to time reformers succeed in overthrowing a corrupt regime, but the struggle involved inevitably is difficult, even dangerous (see chapters 8 and 9).

MEMBERS AND MEETINGS

For almost all members "the union" is the local, not the international. However, only a small group of members—about

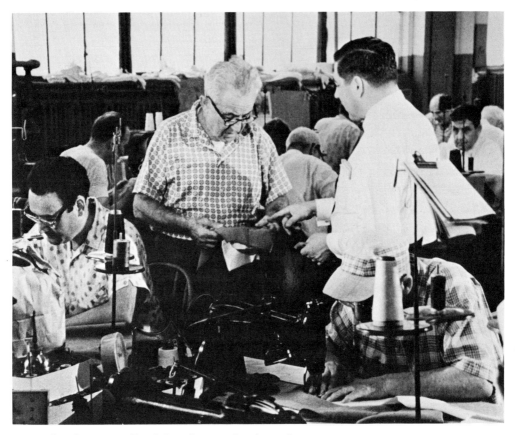

*A local union official (in shirt and tie) works
out a problem with the manager of a garment shop.*

one in ten, it is estimated—become deeply involved in union affairs. Usually these include the men and women who helped organize the local. But it also may include others who see in the union a chance to achieve a sense of belonging and status that otherwise they could not have. They attend the union's meetings regularly, support its goals, work on its programs, participate in its social functions, and know its history and lore. A number become officers. Some even move on to full-time careers with their international unions.

But most are not so close to their union as members were in the past. The major reason is that they need the union less. They may be better educated, work for more enlightened employers, have larger incomes, or lead fuller lives. But often the unions themselves are responsible for this lack of interest. Some are warm, vital, lively organizations which encourage their members to participate. But in others members feel powerless to affect union policies. In some cases an international union may so tightly control its locals that meetings are a meaningless ritual. In others a local may be controlled by a group of officers who regard it as their personal club and, to retain power, actively discourage participation. For example, there are unions where the right to dissent is not always respected. Debate may be cut off if there is "too much" disagreement. Moreover, a member who is repeatedly at odds with the majority may not be tolerated. He may be shouted down or ostracized, he may not be given help with grievances on the job, or, if he is in a craft union, he may be given the poorest assignments. There also are cases when a local is so large it is hard for an individual to have an impact. Confronted with such situations, some members feel they are caught between two bureaucracies—their employer on one side and their union on the other.

Whatever the reason, most members rarely attend the meetings local unions hold each month. Only when the most important questions are at issue, such as the terms of a contract, a vote on a strike, or a proposal to raise dues, do they turn out in large numbers. In all other cases they leave union affairs to the one in ten.

THE LAW OF THE LOCAL

Many union officials regard the ideal local as "half town-meeting, half army." As they see it, once a course of action has been determined, there is a need for unswerving loyalty. To assure such loyalty, every local union has a code of behavior it expects its members to follow. If they do not, they are penalized. The most serious offenses are conspiracies with management, starting a rival union, and misusing union funds. But there are many others, such as crossing a picket line, working for less than the union wage, distributing union membership lists without permission, and slandering another member. Any member may charge any other with violating these rules.

If the officers decide there may be an infraction, they arrange for a trial, which they frequently conduct themselves, serving as judge, jury, and, at times, prosecutor. Usually a member defends himself or he may call on other members or even an attorney to assist him. If he is found guilty, typically he is reprimanded or fined. Although a fine ordinarily is quite small, it can be quite severe. When, for example, a number of TV newsmen continued to work while their union was on strike, they were fined up to $14,000. In the most extreme cases a member may be suspended or expelled from his union, which, as a result, may deprive him of his job. A member who is found guilty may appeal the verdict to the officers of his international union. If he disagrees with their decision, he then may appeal to the delegates at the union's next convention. But it is there usually that the matter rests.

Local unions long have been criticized for their judicial procedures. Although most decisions may be just, there is nothing to prevent the system from being used unfairly. As some unscrupulous officers have found, it is ideal for removing a troublesome member or for crushing an effort to unseat them. To reduce these hazards the United Auto Workers union has an independent Public Review Board comprised of leading citizens to which a member may turn if he feels he has been treated unfairly. The board's members examine the evidence, then render a final verdict by which the union must abide. However, few other unions, if any, provide this opportunity.

CONTRACTS, GRIEVANCES, BROTHERHOOD

A local union's overriding concern is the job—providing employment when possible, improving a worker's opportunities, and protecting him against abuse by his employer. Some go to great lengths to meet these responsibilities. The craft unions, for example, teach their members the skills they need. They also operate hiring halls where a member is assured of a job if one is to be had. Of course, through collective bargaining, all local unions work to improve wages and working conditions, a process described in chapters 14 and 15. In addition, all deal with a member's problems on the job. To make certain their members are treated fairly, they negotiate a grievance system with management through which complaints of all types are handled. As employers have grown larger and the individual worker inevitably has become less important, this system has come to play a major role in protecting worker's rights. However, it also meets management's needs by bringing problems into the open before they fester and become serious.

Of course, some complaints have little basis in fact. But many others are legitimate. They grow out of errors or thoughtless behavior on the part of supervisors or out of deliberate violations of a contract a union and an employer have negotiated. A factory worker, for example, may not get the overtime to which he is entitled, may not receive a promotion for which he is eligible, or may find that an assembly line is being run faster than has been agreed on, which requires more effort for the same pay. A teacher may feel her principal discrimates against her, and as a result gives her poor assignments. A major league baseball player may be housed in a hotel he feels is less comforbable than his contract promises. A merchant seaman may have complaints

A General Electric worker, right, and his shop steward, center, discuss a complaint with their foreman as the first step in a grievance procedure.

about the food served aboard ship. To outsiders these difficulties may seem minor, but to the men and women affected
they are of considerable importance.

In most local unions the task of handling grievances belongs to a team of shop stewards the members elect to represent them on the job. Usually they are given time off with
pay to handle their duties. If a complaint seems justified, a
steward discusses the problem with the worker's supervisor.
If this does not solve the problem, the dispute moves to a
"second step" at which a higher union official, often a chief
steward, meets with the employer's personnel manager or industrial relations manager. If the problem still cannot be re-
solved, the union president, often with the help of an international representative, tries to work things out with the
plant manager, the superintendent of schools, or whoever
else is in charge.

If the dispute cannot be settled, a professional arbitrator is
called in. He considers all sides of the question, then renders
a verdict both parties agree in advance to accept. In some
cases, in fact, a union and an employer hire a permanent arbitrator who handles all disputes that cannot otherwise be
solved. (At times arbitration also is used to settle disputes in
negotiations over contracts [see chapter 16]). Of course,
the disputes that go to arbitration are by far the most per-
plexing. Indeed, some require the wisdom of a Solomon to
decide.

What Would You Decide?

Each of the job disputes described below had to be settled
by an arbitrator. After considering the evidence in each case,
what decision would you reach? Those the arbitrators made
are described at the end of this chapter.

THE CASE OF THE HAIRY MUSICIAN

Phil sold classified advertising over the counter in a newspaper office. Since he dealt with the public he was well aware of the need for maintaining a pleasing appearance. During his first two years on the job he had no trouble observing the company rule that "hair be neatly combed and conservatively styled." But after he and a few friends formed a rock band, he let his hair grow long and also sported mutton chops. Although his musical sideline did not interfere with his work, his hair style distressed his supervisor. As a result Phil trimmed his hair and also combed it once a day, but the results did not satisfy management.

"I'm a part-time musician," he told his boss, "and my public expects me to look like one."

"Right now you're a full-time musician," his boss declared. "Collect your pay and leave!"

Phil complained to his local union whose president then met with the company's personnel manager. "We agree about the need for a neat appearance," the union official said, "but the company should be reasonable . . . about applying the rule when a man is trying to build a second career that needs a somewhat different image."

"We can't have him looking like a freak," the personnel manager replied.

THE CASE OF THE FRUSTRATED GYM TEACHER

Just before the school year began the man who taught physical education to boys in an elementary school resigned. A woman gym teacher who had been teaching girls in the same school system for three years applied for the job. Although members of the school board admitted she was a good teacher and well qualified, they turned down her application and instead hired a man from outside the system who had but one year of experience. It would be hard to find a replacement for the woman teacher, they said. But they also noted that a man was better suited to teach a gym class of young boys. However, the teachers' union had a contract with the school board under which the board agreed to fill vacancies with qualified teachers on its staff, regardless of their sex. The woman gym teacher charged that the agreement had been violated.

THE CASE OF THE SILENT STOOL PIGEON

The manager of a foundry glanced out of his office window one afternoon to find a worker driving out of the company parking lot. Since there still were forty-five minutes to quitting time, he assumed the man had obtained permission to leave early. But when he checked the time cards, as he did each week, he noticed that the man's card had been punched *after* the normal quitting time rather than before. Clearly one of two workers who had punched out at precisely the same time also had punched out for him. But neither would confess. Nor would the man who left early say who was guilty. In the end he was fired and the other two were laid off for three days without pay.

The local union did not protest the discharge, but it did file a grievance in behalf of the two men who had been laid off. As one of the officials put it, "You can't punish an innocent man. Moreover, you can't punish one for not squealing on the other." But management had a different viewpoint. "Employees have an obligation to cooperate in suppressing dishonesty," the personnel manager said. "If the guilty man had come forward, the other would not have been punished."

Most local unions also help with their members' personal problems. This is in line with a long tradition that has its roots in the sick-and-visiting societies and death-and-benefit societies the early craft unions organized. If a member or someone in his family needs blood, for example, other members of the union give theirs. If he cannot work for a long period, his union may provide him with an income until he can. If he has a problem with alcoholism, mental health, drug addiction, his marriage, or his children, his union will advise him on where to obtain help. In fact, many local unions have members who have been trained by the AFL–CIO to assist their fellow members in finding help. Some of the larger local unions also provide free legal services, special insurance programs, low-interest loans, and discounts on various purchases. Members of several teachers' unions, for example, can buy a new car for only $100 over the list price. The teachers' union in New York even has a travel service which arranges low-cost trips throughout the world.

Almost every local union is also involved in politics. To advance laws they favor they send delegations to meetings of city councils, county boards, and state legislatures. To help candidates they favor, they pay for campaign expenses and organize drives to register sympathetic voters and get them to the polls. (When a candidate for high office is involved, a local union works with its international union and the AFL–CIO [see chapter 18].) Of course, if their man wins they expect his backing for legislation they seek and any favors he can provide. In helping a candidate for mayor, for example, some unions assure themselves of lenient treatment by local police in the event of a strike. If there are more pickets involved than the law permits, if they become unruly, or if there are scuffles between strikers and nonstrikers, under ordinary circumstances members of a local union might be jailed. But when the mayor is in debt to the union, there are cases when the police look the other way.

The cost of running a local union varies greatly with its size, problems, and programs. With over 55,000 members, the United Federation of Teachers in New York has an annual budget of over $1.5 million. With but 300 members, Local 502 of the United Auto Workers, which represents employees in a ball-bearing factory in Trenton, New Jersey, spends less than $10,000 a year.

Once a local union has negotiated its first contract it is likely to have a long life. If its members become dissatisfied, however, they can readily dispense with its services. If 30 per cent agree, usually a government agency will conduct a referendum on the issue in which all members may vote. If a majority decides to "decertify" the local, it loses its standing as a bargaining agent. But very few suffer this fate. The year this was written only 234 out of over 80,000 local unions were challenged. Of these, but 165 were voted out.

What Did You Decide?

These were the arbitrators' decisions in the job disputes described earlier in this chapter.

THE CASE OF THE HAIRY MUSICIAN

The arbitrator agreed with the company that Phil should have been fired. Phil could wear his hair any way he wished. But if he chose to wear it as a musician did, then he made himself unemployable as an over-the-counter classified ad salesman.

THE CASE OF THE FRUSTRATED GYM TEACHER

The arbitrator concluded that the woman gym teacher had been denied the job as a boys' gym teacher because of her sex. Rather than cause the male teacher who had been hired to lose his job, he decided that the woman be given the assignment at the earliest practical time, but no later than the start of the next school year.

THE CASE OF THE SILENT STOOL PIGEON

The arbitrator decided that neither of the men the company had laid off could be punished, for it could not prove which had punched out for the worker who had left early.

8 | The Rank and File

Although there are over 20 million members of the rank and file (a military term labor leaders like to use to describe the great mass of union members), the statisticians know a good deal about them. For example:

> Eighty per cent are men.
> Eighty-eight per cent are white.
> Seventy-five per cent are over thirty years of age; fifty per cent are over forty.
> Over half live in one of six states: New York, Pennsylvania, Ohio, Michigan, Illinois, California.

Despite these similarities union members are as diverse as the nation itself. They include suburbanites, city dwellers, Republicans, Democrats, reactionaries, liberals, Jews, Christians, college graduates, illiterates, the well-to-do, and the poorest of the poor. Some pick grapes for a living. Others pound nails. Others fly jetliners or play in symphony orchestras.

A number form unions on their own. Others join existing unions. In either case they become members for economic reasons or for social reasons or because their fellow workers ostracize them or threaten them if they do not join or because their families have been unionists for generations. However, the largest number have no choice. As we have seen, they must join a union if they want a particular job. Inevitably these great differences affect the attitudes workers have toward their unions, which range from deep affection and loyalty to extreme distaste.

"THEY" AND "WE"

Many union members know little about modern unionism, and most know even less about the labor movement's earlier struggles and achievements, which some old-timers find exasperating. "When people get their first jobs," one observed, "they think that all the benefits they get are the company's idea. Like hell! We had to fight to get them! We had to contend! And they wouldn't exist if it weren't for the union."

Although the average unionist may not know or care very much about the past, he is very much concerned about what his union can do for him now. Researchers find that he sees his union not as a brotherhood of workers involved in a class struggle, but as a service organization which for a monthly fee protects him against unfair treatment. In fact, when he thinks of his union at all, he is likely to think of it as an organization with which he has no intimate connection, as *they*, not as *we*. Some labor leaders call such unionists "slot-machine members." As one explained, "They drop their dues in the slot each month, and every year or two they expect to hit the jackpot. If they don't, they get mad and shake the machine." When a crisis arises, however, such as a strike, most are willing to help. They may not feel close to their union, but they recognize that they depend on it. It is at such times, indeed, that *they* frequently becomes *we*.

MIDDLE-AGED WHITE MEN AND OTHER MEMBERS

Not too many years ago the typical union member was a middle-aged white man who worked in a factory or on a construction job. Due to changes in the economy, today an increasing number of union members are service workers in hospitals, hotels, and restaurants, white collar workers in stores and offices, and technicians and professionals (see chapter 2). Moreover, a growing number are young people, women, and members of racial minorities. Together they are having a growing impact on the character of the labor movement.

YOUNG PEOPLE

One of the delegates to a recent national convention of the United Auto Workers was a seventeen-year-old girl who worked in a factory in Kitchener, Ontario, and was recording secretary of her local union. It is estimated that one union member in four today is in his teens or twenties, and the proportion is growing. In some unions as many as 40 per cent of the members are young people. Never before have there been so many. However, most do not join out of a deep interest in unionism. Their numbers reflect in part their growth in the population. In addition, there are a great many union shop agreements under which they must become members, whether or not they want to (see chapter 7).

Labor leaders tend to feel uneasy about this group. When they discuss younger members they sound like fathers discussing their teen-age children. They are sure that eventually they will turn out all right, but there *are* problems. One they cite is that young people do not know anything about unions, which they blame on the schools. Another is that younger members tend to think more like managers than like workers and have little loyalty to the ideas for which labor stands, which they also blame on the schools (see chapter 12). Still another is that many do not always follow their leaders, which is the greatest cause of concern. In recent years one collective bargaining agreement in eight has been turned down by the rank and file, although in the past rarely was there a rejection. Some union leaders place much of the blame for this on young militants they regard as irresponsible. As one official put it, "They strike at the drop of a hat—and at times endanger their jobs and those of others. But the way they see it they can always get another job. . . ."

To explain the union movement to its younger members, and to build their loyalty, the AFL–CIO and various international unions conduct courses, prepare films, and publish materials of various types, but as union education directors admit, the kind of allegiance they hope for is not easy to achieve.

WOMEN

Most of the 4 million women in the labor movement are clustered in about 20 international unions. These include the garment unions, where 80 per cent of the members are women, the teachers' unions, the Communications Workers, the Auto Workers, the Hotel and Restaurant Workers, the Retail Clerks, and the Electrical Workers. Labor officials say that women make good unionists, that often they are more loyal and more militant than men. But even when they comprise a majority they tend to have far less influence in union affairs than men do. The Electrical Workers union is typical. A third of its members are women, yet in a recent year only 18 of its 600 locals had women as presidents. Women have even less representation on the national level. In the Amalgamated Clothing Workers of America, 280,000 members out of 380,000 are women, yet when this was written the Amalgamated's Executive Board consisted of 26 men, but no women. Even in unions of professional workers, where members have more education and women have more power, the dominance of the male is a fact of life.

However, the economic discrimination a working woman faces is an even more serious problem. She may be limited to certain jobs, receive less pay than a man for equivalent work, have fewer opportunities for advancement, and be more subject to layoff in the event that work is in short supply. A number of laws ban economic discrimination because of sex, but in one guise or another it persists. Some unions vigorously fight such discrimination. The Transport Workers Union, for example, successfully ended discrimination against the airline stewardesses it represents. American Airlines had insisted its stewardesses retire when they reached the age of thirty-two, or earlier if they married, arguing that either event left them less attractive to customers, most of whom are males. Now a stewardess may keep her job as long as other employees are able to keep theirs. However, many unions do little about discrimination against their women members. With their predominantly male leadership, such problems have low priority.

When their unions fail them, the most determined women have turned for help to NOW, the National Organization for Women, which has spearheaded the Women's Liberation Movement in the United States. NOW will meet with employers, picket their plants and offices if it seems necessary, and even go to court, suing employers who discriminate and unions that cooperate in discrimination. However, most working women pay their dues and accept things as they are.

RACIAL MINORITIES

Some 2.5 million blacks, Spanish–Americans, and other non-whites hold union cards. Together they represent about 2 per cent of union members. Through their membership, many have escaped from poverty and have acquired some control over the forces that affect their lives. The men and women who work in the soup kitchens in Camden, New Jersey, the garbage collectors in Memphis, and the grape pickers in California are but a few examples. They also have benefited from laws for which the labor movement has fought, particularly those that prohibit racial discrimination, set minimum wages, and finance improvements in urban life. It would seem from this that there would be a close relationship between the unions, which traditionally have helped the underdog, and racial minorities. But the relationship varies widely from one segment of the labor movement to another. Although the AFL–CIO and many individual unions have close ties to such groups, there are others, particularly at the local level, where rivalry, suspicion, and hostility mark the relationship between one race and another.

Early in this century there were virtually no racial minorities in the unions. When the Urban League, today a leading civil rights organization, tried to get work for unemployed blacks, it got them jobs as strikebreakers. The great steel strike of 1919, in which 300,000 workers struck for union recognition, was broken with the help of black men. In fact, when nonwhites finally began entering the labor movement in the 1930s, only some unions welcomed them on an equal basis. A number would grant them membership if they joined segregated locals so as not to discourage whites from joining. Still others would not admit them under any circumstances.

After twenty years a score of international unions still refused to admit nonwhites. Moreover, there still were over six hundred segregated local unions, most of which were in the South. Under the prodding of A. Philip Randolph, then president of the all-black Brotherhood of Sleeping Car Porters, the AFL–CIO finally took steps to eliminate these injustices. International unions with "whites only" restrictions agreed to open their doors to all who qualified regardless of the color of their skin, and those with segregated locals agreed to integrate them.

Although these were important improvements, putting them to work was not easy. By 1970, 150 local unions still had not been integrated. Moreover, many unions in the building trades still were virtually "lily white." Since these unions trained most of the nation's craftsmen, and thereby controlled most of the construction jobs, most skilled construction workers were white.

Even with the passage of the Civil Rights Act of 1964 and the announcement of ambitious programs by these unions to recruit nonwhites, change came slowly. In the Boilermakers union, for example, 5.5 per cent of the membership was black at this writing; in the Electrical Workers, it was 1.9 per cent; in the Iron Workers, it was 1.7 per cent; in the Plumbers it was 0.8 per cent; in the Carpenters it was 2.9 per cent.[*]

Impatient over this slow progress, thousands of unemployed blacks and Puerto Ricans demonstrated at construction sites in New York, Pittsburgh, Chicago, and other cities, demanding jobs. In some cases they disrupted work in progress. At times they also clashed with white unionists. White workers, in turn, also demonstrated. In Pittsburgh, for example, they marched through the business district in their hard hats and coveralls chanting "Wallace! Wallace! Wallace!" for George Wallace, the Alabama politician who symbolized opposition to racial equality.

In this period black workers already in unions began to voice demands for more power, much as Jews, Italians, Poles, and other minorities had done in earlier days. Within the Transport Workers Union, black members formed the Rank and File Transit Workers to push for the election of black officers. Within the United Auto Workers, several organizations emerged including the Dodge Revolutionary Union Movement. Within the steel, hotel, freight, garment, and utility unions, still other "black caucuses" appeared. Their potential strength was reflected in a struggle between the Retail, Wholesale and Department Store Union and the union's District 65 in New York where half the 30,000 members were black or Spanish–American. District 65 demanded that nonwhites be given high-ranking posts at international headquarters and that a major effort be made to organize members of racial minorities. When the international union

---

[*] *New York Times,* February 9, 1971.

Unemployed black workers protest their exclusion from a building trades union, and thus from construction jobs.

did not meet these demands, the district seceded and created a new international union, the National Council of Distributive Workers of America.

In one New York union, however, neither a black caucus nor a new union was needed. During its first twenty-five years Local 1199, Drug and Hospital Union, was primarily an organization of white Jewish pharmacists. But in 1958, with their struggles behind them, they took a fateful step. That year the union began to organize the unskilled black and Puerto Rican workers who cleaned the rooms, prepared the food, and helped care for the patients at hospitals throughout the city. There were thousands who earned as little as $32 for a forty-four-hour week, had no benefits, and could not obtain a hearing for their grievances. Even though they had full-time jobs, many needed welfare payments to make ends meet.

When this was written, almost fifteen years had passed and there had been changes. A hospital worker in New York earned $130 a week instead of $32. He now received the kinds of benefits most workers took for granted. He also had a formal grievance system which assured that his complaints would be given a fair hearing. He also had a union that had given him power and pride he had not known before. As one hospital worker said, "The union helped me realize how important I am as a person, which before I'm afraid I didn't quite realize. . . ."

As far as the union was concerned, it had grown eight times, from 5000 members to 40,000. It had changed from an organization of college-educated whites to a union of unskilled blacks and Puerto Ricans, most of whom had not finished high school. Its leadership also had changed. Leon Davis, the bearded pharmacist who had led the union from the beginning, still was president. But the officers now included men and women who once were diet clerks, floor moppers, and dishwashers.

The union's goals also had changed. Once these had been purely economic. Now the objective was to make the union a way of life. It provided free legal advice, information on where to find good housing, and help with personal problems. It also had forged a strong alliance with the civil rights movement, winning the backing of black leaders like Martin Luther King, Jr., and of white liberals who saw the union as a means to build equality and dignity for racial minorities.

In the process it had acquired an intensely loyal and militant membership. At a union meeting one rainy night not too long ago, Leon Davis put it this way: "We have brought together in our union people who were nobodies and now are somebodies." Everyone there, black and white, stood together and cheered.

9 | Racketeers and Reformers

Most unions have trustworthy, dedicated officers who put in long hours at a difficult job. But there also are unions with dishonest leaders who use their power for personal gain. They are relatively few when the entire labor movement is considered, but they affect hundreds of thousands of workers. Some are union officials who succumb to temptation. Others are professional racketeers, including members of the Mafia, who work in partnership with labor leaders or even operate unions of their own.

In all cases the objective is money, and for the unscupulous there are many ways to obtain it. Often they steal from union funds with which they have been entrusted. They also rely on bribes from employers. For a fee they are willing to negotiate a lenient contract, look the other way when the contract is violated, and guarantee an employer freedom from strikes. If he is willing to pay enough, they even may arrange to create labor problems for his competitors.

Of course, a member can complain about corruption, oppose corrupt officers in an election, or turn to the law for help, but in each case there are hazards. He could be fired from his job. He could be threatened with violence, or he could be beaten—or worse. A business agent who testified on illegal dealings in his union was severely flogged with guns and a blackjack in the basement of his union hall. An informant in another union had his legs broken in an elevator as the car repeatedly traveled from the basement to the roof and back again.

However, law-enforcement officials say that crooked labor leaders are not the only ones responsible for corruption. They criticize businessmen who deal with racketeers. They criticize others who turn down "deals" but do not report the crooks who approached them. They blame the AFL–CIO, which, they say, is reluctant to use its power against corruption. They also blame union members for leaving union affairs to their officers and "looking the other way" to avoid trouble. At times, courageous members try to free their unions from corruption, but they are the exceptions and, as we have seen, there are hazards.

CORRUPTION IN THE TEAMSTERS

Labor racketeers first broke into the headlines in the 1950s when a Congressional committee set out to determine the extent of corruption in labor relations and what could be done about it. A stern, conservative Senator from Arkansas, John McClellan, was chairman of the committee. A young millionaire, Robert F. Kennedy, was its chief attorney. Their investigation turned out to be one of the longest in Congressional history, extending over two and a half years. In this period they interviewed 1500 unionists and businessmen whose testimony was as shocking as any ever given before such a committee.

The McClellan Committee devoted much of its attention to the International Brotherhood of Teamsters and its leaders, Dave Beck, who was president when the investigation began, and James R. (Jimmy) Hoffa, who succeeded him. (Hoffa is testifying in the photograph at the beginning of the chapter.) The Teamsters union was at the time the largest, wealthiest and most powerful union in the country, just as it is today. With almost all the truck drivers and warehouse workers as members, it literally controlled the food, clothing, and other necessities without which the nation could not function.

The committee found that Beck, Hoffa, and their assistants had misused almost $10 million in Teamster funds and had exercised tyrannical control over other union officials, union members, and many employers with whom they had contracts. To keep "troublemakers" in line, they relied on "goons" who specialized in beatings, bombings, dynamitings, and other strong-arm tactics. To keep local unions tightly under control, they replaced uncooperative officers with "trustees," officials from the international union who ran things to suit Hoffa or Beck. At one point over a hundred local unions were under such supervision. To keep outside interference to a minimum, the two regularly bribed politicians, judges, police chiefs, and other public officials.

Meanwhile, Beck and Hoffa fattened their incomes with bribes from employers, rewards for Teamster business they gave to cooperative firms, and "fees" for loans they made from Teamster funds to businessmen who were poor credit risks and had trouble borrowing money elsewhere. In addition, they used the union's money as if it were their own. For example, Beck provided himself with $43 shirts, $14 ties, freezers, boats, a race horse, a trainer, a jockey, and a house in an exclusive section of Seattle, which he not only built with union funds but later sold to the union for $163,000!

Beck, Hoffa, and scores of other Teamster officials were charged by Federal grand juries with a wide range of crimes and eventually were found guilty and jailed. Ironically they spent another $700,000 in Teamster funds to defend themselves. While they were in prison, moreover, it was their loyal associates, rather than reformers, who ran the union. Nor was the membership particularly outraged. Their attitude seemed to be, "They got us good contracts and were entitled to something for themselves." In fact, while Hoffa languished in prison, he still was regarded as the union's president and his wife represented him at important union functions. But finally he resigned, and soon after he was paroled on the condition that he would not attempt to influence the policies of the Teamsters or any other union for eight years more.

The committee also found evidence of corruption in a number of other unions. In addition, it discovered that over fifty companies, including some that were nationally known, had engaged in questionable behavior in their dealings with unions. Some had resorted to bribery to gain advantages. Others had relied on so-called labor relations consultants who used unethical, even illegal, methods to thwart union organizing campaigns. An official of Sears Roebuck and

Company, for example, testified that his firm had spent almost $250,000 in a four-year period for the services of such a consultant. He called these efforts "inexcusable, unnecessary and disgraceful. . . . A repetition of these mistakes will *not* be tolerated by this company. . . ." he told the committee.*

Labor's top officials opposed the investigation by the McClellan Committee, fearing that the reputation of the entire union movement would be severely damaged when the actions of a small minority were publicized. But when it appeared that Congress might take steps to regulate unions more closely, the AFL–CIO took steps to clean house. It adopted a code of ethical practices that unions within the federation were expected to follow. It also conducted its own hearings in which it charged eight unions with corrupt practices. Five took steps to reform themselves, but three refused to cooperate and were expelled. They included the Bakery Workers, the Laundry Workers, and the Teamsters, which alone represented 10 per cent of the nation's union members. But, the business executives who had been involved—"the respectables," as Robert Kennedy called them—kept their jobs, and the companies they represented continued as members in good standing of the National Association of Manufacturers, the Chamber of Commerce of the United States, and other groups that comprise the business establishment.

Despite its efforts to clean house, the AFL–CIO could not forestall tighter controls by the government. The Landrum–Griffin Act (officially the Labor–Management Reporting and Disclosure Act) now regulates union elections, combats the misuse of union funds, and oversees expenditures by business firms for labor relations consultants and other techniques to combat unionism. To protect union members, it also established a Bill of Rights which deals with the rights and re-

---

* *New York Times,* October 26, 1957.

sponsibilities of unions and their members in their relationships. As a result of all these actions, corruption within unions was reduced. But it was not eliminated.

MAKING THE SCORE

In the following telephone conversation transcribed by the Federal Bureau of Investigation, three members of the Mafia in New Jersey are discussing a new "racket union" they plan to set up in a factory in New York.

CORKY: What are the dues a month?

JOE: Well, you can make yours five dollars, but I have only four [in my union].

CORKY: And what is the initiation fee? . . .

JOE: . . . You could charge $25, $50, or $75—whatever you want. Why not $10 now and anybody that comes in after that $25?

CORKY: All right.

SAM: Well, how are you going to make a score if you're so cheap?

CORKY: Well . . . when I sit down with the boss [in the factory], I'll tell him how much it's gonna cost . . . in welfare, hospitalization, and all that. . . . Then I'll say, "Let's cut it in half and forget about it. . . ." I'll show first what it's going to cost—then [I'll show him] how much I'm gonna save [him by letting him ignore these benefits].

SAM: Well, you have to organize the plant so that nobody else walks in there—then you wind up with the dues every month. That's $300 a month. You could do that?

JOE: Sure. He could give you a solid contract for three years. . . .

SAM: Then you could get a pay every year. . . .*

---

* *New York Times,* June 13, 1969.

Racket unions are unions their members never asked for. In fact, frequently they do not know they are members until dues are taken from their paychecks. Typically there are no meetings, the members have nothing to say about how the union is run, they receive no protection from abuses by management, and they are saddled with poor contracts. Most of the racket unions are in New York, Philadelphia, Baltimore, Chicago, and other large cities. They function in gas stations, car washes, small factories, and other businesses whose owners operate on a shoestring. Their members invariably are black or Spanish–American workers who are new to city life, badly need their jobs, and do not know what their rights are. Their "officers" are racketeers operating on their own or as part of the Mafia or some other organized group.

When a racketeer decides to "organize" a "union" usually he offers an employer a "sweetheart contract" which sets wages and benefits at a minimum level. He also agrees to keep out legitimate unions which would demand a far better contract and thereby increase costs. In return, he wants a large fee from the employer and a monthly dues payment from each employee. If an employer agrees to go along, he pressures his employees into signing the necessary papers or forges their signatures. He then begins deducting dues from their pay which he turns over to their "officers." If an employer resists, he may be faced with violence. If a worker resists, he is likely to be fired. But because most of the workers involved do not know any better or are afraid, they seldom complain, even though they are cheated of a decent wage.

The police have great difficulty in stopping such practices. If the workers agree to accept a "union," the law recognizes it as their representative, no matter how undemocratic or ineffective it may be. Even when racketeers move in without the workers' consent, little can be done unless they complain or band together and reject the "union," but usually most are too frightened to try.

At the urging of the AFL–CIO, a number of international unions have tried to help such workers break away and form real unions. A few have been successful, but when hoodlums intervene it is not easy. The long-term solution, as the AFL–CIO sees it, lies in teaching workers new to city life what their rights are so that they can avoid such traps. In New York a member of the federation's staff was spending full time on this. Yet the problem of the worker already in a racket union remains. When this was written, there were 40,000 such men and women in New York alone.

"YOU WILL BE PROUD TO BE A PAINTER!"

At times legitimate unions also turn bad despite Federal regulations, but usually their members know their rights and in some cases they fight back. This happened in Painters District Council 9, which bargained for twenty-seven local unions in New York. When Martin Rarback was elected secretary–treasurer of the Council, its highest office, its 13,-000 members were paid more than any other painters or paperhangers in the country. When he was turned out of office twenty years later, they were third from the bottom of the list. In the years between he connived with labor racketeers, negotiated sweetheart contracts, ignored the members' grievances, and swelled his income with bribes from employers.

Those who opposed him when he stood for re-election found it a fruitless exercise. They were not permitted to speak at meetings of the local unions, nor could they obtain the members' names to contact them by mail. Moreover,

Rarback won every election, no matter what the vote. In fact, if a member became too troublesome, he would find himself without a job. A small group of rebels led by a painter named Frank Schonfeld received this treatment. But instead of giving up they continued to fight. Through newsletters, bulletins, and secret meetings with other members, they slowly built a following. As if to underscore the importance of their effort, the latest contract Rarback had negotiated had provided a raise of four cents an hour.

When the district attorney's office began to investigate Rarback's activities, with the help of Schonfeld and other members, the tide began to turn. When Rarback was charged with accepting $840,000 in bribes, Schonfeld decided that the time had come to run for secretary–treasurer. Although he was awaiting trial, Rarback decided to oppose him. But this time he was defeated decisively. Two months later, moreover, he was convicted and jailed.

When Schonfeld moved into his new office after the election, he found in a desk drawer six .38 caliber bullets, a reminder of the old days, but also perhaps a warning of difficulties ahead. The following month he called the Council's first general membership meeting in fourteen years. Over 3000 painters and paperhangers jammed a Manhattan auditorium to hear him speak.

"This union belongs to you," he declared. "It is not my private property. . . . I will not be silent if anyone's democratic rights are violated or if anyone sabotages your decisions. . . . We will build a painters' union that is respected by the employers, by the public, and by the labor movement. You will be proud to be a painter!"

The following year he negotiated a new agreement with the employers. The raise he won came to $1.40 an hour— $1.36 more than Rarback willingly had accepted three years before.

Part Three | FRIENDS AND ENEMIES

A union does not exist in a vacuum. It is part of a complex web of relationships. It affects and is affected in varying degrees by the employers with whom it deals or hopes to deal, the various governments and their branches, and the public. In each group it has friends and enemies.

10 | Management

Most employers do not regard unions with affection. They
see them as a disruptive force which slows their operations,
weakens their relationships with their employees, threatens
their profits, and, above all, limits their freedom to manage
as they see fit. As a result, most do not welcome a union's efforts to organize their workers. In fact, some use every means
at their command to fight the formation of new unions (see
chapter 13). But if these efforts fail and a new local is
formed, the relationship that results varies widely.

In some cases it is marked by intense hostility. To comply
with the law, an employer may recognize a union, but he
also may refuse to bargain seriously or to cooperate in other
ways. He even may try to undermine the union and ulti-

mately destroy it. One common tactic is to provoke a strike, then hire nonunion workers to replace the strikers. The textile unions regularly encounter opposition of this kind in the South.

However, most employers accept a union as a fact of life. Some remain convinced that it is nothing but a source of trouble, but others come to see advantages in the situation. One is the grievance procedure, which makes it easier to identify problems before they become too serious (see chapter 7). Another is the responsibility a union assumes for enforcing many of the rules that regulate work procedures. Another is improved communication with employees. Many workers do not fully trust their employers, but when union officers accept a company's actions and explanations, usually the workers go along.

Due to the nature of their businesses, a number of employers develop close relationships with unions that represent their workers. In fact, some cannot function effectively without a union's help. This is true, for example, of many building contractors who rely on skilled craftsmen. It also is the case with maritime companies and garment manufacturers and major producers of plays. Typically the company and the union form an economic alliance. The employer provides jobs and good working conditions and frequently the funds to train workers in the skills they need. The unions provide the workers and the training and see to it that high standards are maintained.

Such a partnership also may extend to other matters. To protect jobs and keep salaries high, some unions do what they can to keep their industries prosperous. The garment unions and the glass blowers' union advertise to promote the products their members create. One of the unions in the printing trades publishes a beautiful quarterly magazine,

Lithopinion, to demonstrate the quality of printing that can be achieved with lithography, the method its members use. When business is slow some unions also use their influence in Washington to obtain government contracts for companies that employ their members and thereby forestall layoffs. At the Machinists union, a staff member works full time at this.

Some employers have contracts with but a single union. However, many deal with a dozen or more, each of which represents a different occupational group. The Union Carbide Corporation, for example, has contracts with twenty-five different unions. In a small firm the owner may handle grievances, bargaining, and other matters involving labor relations, frequently with the help of an attorney. In a school district the Board of Education deals with unions. In a small city the mayor does. In a large city an industrial relations expert handles the job. In a large corporation an industrial relations department is responsible. The United States Steel Corporation, for example, has more than a hundred specialists at its corporate headquarters who devote their time to union matters. In addition, each of its steel mills has its own industrial relations manager.

The conflict between unions and management also extends to Congress and the state legislatures, where the rules that govern labor relations are established. Since such legislation has an important impact on how successful unions are, both sides make strenuous efforts to obtain laws that meet their needs. They finance propaganda campaigns to influence public attitudes, work to elect candidates who are sympathetic to their cause, and lobby vigorously.

To carry out its fight, the labor movement relies on a coalition that includes the AFL–CIO, the state labor federations, the major unions, a variety of liberal organizations, and a large corps of liberal politicians. Management relies on a coalition that includes, among others, the National Association of Manufacturers, the Chamber of Commerce of the United States, major companies, trade associations, and a great many conservative politicians. The struggle between these forces is as old as the labor movement itself, but in modern times, as we shall see, it has grown in intensity and importance (see chapters 11–18).

11 | The Government

Officials of labor and management agree on at least one point. They would be happier if the Federal government were less concerned with their affairs. But there is little chance of that. In a society as complex as ours, relations between labor and management have an important impact on the nation, with the result that the government sees no alternative but to become involved. As long as serious problems do not arise, it plays a minor role. But when there is strife that affects the public or when the rights of an individual are affected, the government is likely to intervene. Thus, it may enforce the right of a worker to join a union. It may require that an employer recognize a union and bargain with it over terms of employment. If a deadlock in bargaining develops, it may provide a mediator to help solve the problem, or if the situation is serious enough, it may even impose a solution of its own.

Four Federal agencies are directly concerned with labor–management relations. The National Labor Relations Board oversees the formation of new unions and regulates the conditions under which they bargain with management. The National Mediation Board deals with bargaining deadlocks in the transportation industry. The Federal Mediation and Conciliation Service does the same elsewhere in the economy. In addition, the Labor–Management Services Administration works to prevent corruption in relationships between the two sides. Three other government units also are involved. The Department of Labor determines whether additional supervision or other changes are needed. Committees in the House of Representatives and the United States Senate have similar responsibilities. In all, the Federal government employs more than 5000 people and spends over $50 million a year to carry out these activities. But it was not always this way.

TAKE IT OR LEAVE IT

For many years the government stood aloof from labor relations. Except for a severe crisis, it ignored conflicts over formation of unions, breakdowns in bargaining, strikes, and other problems. It did so on the theory that it was best for labor and management to work things out on their own. But there was a flaw in this reasoning. Employers and employees were not equally matched. Since an individual worker had virtually no bargaining power, usually the employer had his way. A worker could try to form a union, but it was not easy. Employees who showed any interest often were fired. In fact, many employers required that a worker sign a yellow dog contract when he was hired in which, as we have seen, he agreed not to join a union. Even if a union were organized and a majority of the workers joined, their employer was not obliged to deal with it. If they tried to force him to do so by striking, he could turn to the courts for an order requiring that they return to work. And usually he got the help he needed.

It was not until the great economic depression of the 1930s that the government's role changed (see chapter 3). When 13 million jobs were wiped out, whatever bargaining power a worker had also disappeared. If he did not accept the pay and working conditions he was offered, someone else was only too glad to do so. Even a union was not much help, for most employers were in such a strong position they saw no need to bargain. As a rising number of workers competed for a shrinking number of jobs, inevitably wages fell and with them the purchasing power the nation needed so badly to get moving again. The nation's leaders also were deeply troubled by growing frustration and unrest among workers, which they feared could lead only to political upheaval.

As discussed earlier, one solution many saw was the development of strong unions. They reasoned that the spread of unionism would help raise wages, increase purchasing power, extend democracy on the job, and, as a result, defuse unrest. Over vigorous opposition from the business community, Congress passed the needed legislation and for the first time the Federal government acquired a major role in labor relations.

THE FRAMEWORK

The Norris–La Guardia Act of 1932. This was the first of the laws Congress passed. It prohibited use of the yellow dog contracts discussed earlier and reduced the power of Federal courts to ban or limit strikes and picketing.

The National Labor Relations Act of 1935. Also known as the *Wagner Act,* this law replaced one that earlier had been declared unconstitutional. Labor leaders call the Wagner Act their "Magna Charta" and for good reason. It guaranteed workers the right to form unions and required that employers bargain with them in good faith (see chapter 3). It also prohibited a list of "unfair labor practices" by management. Most important, management could no longer interfere with the establishment of a union and could not fire a worker if he joined.

To administer the Wagner Act Congress created the National Labor Relations Board—the NLRB, as it is usually called. The agency has two responsibilities. One is to determine whether the employees at a particular organization want a union to represent them. When a union submits proof that 30 per cent of the employees involved already have joined, the NLRB conducts an election at which everyone involved may vote. If a majority vote for the union, it becomes the bargaining agent for all the workers involved. In an ordinary year the NLRB supervises over 12,000 such elections.

The agency's other job is to enforce the ban against unfair labor practices. In this case it functions like a labor court. If a complaint cannot be settled "out of court," a trial examiner conducts a hearing at which both sides testify. He then weighs the evidence, reaches a decision, and, if warranted, imposes a penalty. Ordinarily an offender must stop his illegal activity, rehire anyone who has lost his job as a result, and pay him damages. In a typical year the agency's trial examiners conduct more than 15,000 hearings. If either party is dissatisfied with a decision, it may appeal to the five commis-

Workers in a Seattle plant vote on whether to have a union.

sioners who head the NLRB. In addition, it may appeal their decision to a Federal court and, if it wishes, to the United States Supreme Court (see chapter 13).

As noted earlier, the Wagner Act had an extraordinary effect. With the restraints placed on management, unions grew at a remarkable pace. In addition, with greater bargaining power, workers earned more, spent more, and had more of a voice in their jobs, with the result that unrest diminished. However, many businessmen and many lawmakers were not enthusiastic about the Wagner Act. They felt it was one-sided and left management at a disadvantage. As they saw it there was a need for a more just balance of power. The result was still another crucial law.

The Labor–Management Relations Act of 1947. This legislation is better known as the *Taft–Hartley Act.* It signifi-

cantly strengthened the hand of an employer who opposed unionism. It permitted him to argue against the formation of a union by his employees, made it easier to stop strikes and picketing, and for the first time held unions accountable for various unfair labor practices, just as the Wagner Act had done with management. For example, now a union also had to bargain in good faith. Moreover, it could not threaten a worker because he refused to join, nor could it force his employer to fire him for this reason. Nor could it use a "secondary boycott" as a weapon through which it forced a neutral company to stop doing business with a firm with which it had a dispute. The new law also banned the closed shop, under which only union members could be hired. It also permitted individual states to ban union security agreements on which labor relies to maintain its strength (see chapter 7). There also were other restrictions, all of which led union officials to brand the Taft–Hartley Act as a "slave labor law" and fight for its repeal. However, they failed and it has remained in force.

The Labor–Management Reporting and Disclosure Act of 1959, also known as the *Landrum–Griffin Act.* As discussed in chapter 8, this law was designed to reduce corruption in labor–management relations. It regulates union elections, oversees union finances, and in other ways tries to protect a member's rights against unscrupulous labor leaders and employers.

DOES IT WORK?

The guarantees set forth in these laws and the government agencies that enforce them are the framework on which our system of industrial relations rests. But when this was written both sides were dissatisfied with the framework. The unions were troubled by the time it took to obtain a decision regarding an unfair labor practice by management. Months might elapse—even a year or more—before a case was settled. They also were troubled by the penalties imposed. Rarely were they severe enough to discourage future violations. In fact, the advantage some firms gained from firing employees who joined unions or from violating the law in other ways far outweighed the penalties they suffered. As a result, labor wanted the framework strengthened.

Management sought even more drastic changes. Its representatives at the National Association of Manufacturers and the Chamber of Commerce charged that the National Labor Relations Board was prolabor, and that its decisions gave unions far more power than Congress had intended. Although the NLRB disagreed, the two business organizations mounted an ambitious drive to "reform" or replace the agency and to reverse "antimanagement" decisions it had made. Whether either side would succeed remained to be seen.

LABOR RELATIONS AND THE STATES

Federal laws do not apply to everyone. For all sorts of reasons—many selfish, a few practical—a number of groups were not included. At this writing, farm workers are excluded due to the opposition of farm organizations. Many government workers also are excluded. So are employees in nonprofit hospitals and domestic servants. So are workers whose employers operate a primarily local business. In such situations a state may or may not closely regulate labor relations.

In the 1970s only one state in four guaranteed such workers the right to join a union, required that their employers bargain with their union, and provided protection against unfair labor practices.* In all others, an employer was not legally obliged to deal with a union, even if every employee was a member. Whether he did so usually depended on the strength of the union, the test of which usually was a strike.

Two other major conflicts also involved the states. One related to the ban on union security agreements discussed in chapter 7. The other concerned the right of government employees to join unions and to strike. This conflict is discussed in chapters 15 and 16.

---

* Colorado, Connecticut, Hawaii, Kansas, Massachusetts, Michigan, Minnesota, New York, North Dakota, Pennsylvania, Rhode Island, Utah, Wisconsin.

12 | The Public

When I asked 120 high school students how they felt about
unions, 80 per cent said they were essential to the welfare of
the workers in this country. Researchers find that most
Americans feel this way. But they also find that a great many
are not enthusiastic about unions. Despite what unions have
accomplished, the public tends to distrust them, even fear
them. When researchers from Cornell University interviewed social studies teachers, for example, almost three
teachers in five said that unions had too much power. When
interviewers from the Gallup Poll asked a nationwide sample
which institution was the biggest threat to the country, one
person in four named the labor movement.

Some labor leaders are not troubled by such attitudes.

Their reaction was reflected in a comment by Teamster leader Jimmy Hoffa. As he told an interviewer, "Who gives a damn what the public thinks?" But many labor leaders are deeply concerned by what the public thinks. They say that many of the public's attitudes are incorrect and are based on ignorance, misunderstanding, and a tendency to regard all unions as the same, when in fact unions differ markedly.

"IF MY GRANDFATHER COULD DO IT, THEY CAN DO IT"

The public's attitudes toward labor unions are influenced by a number of factors. One of the most important is how much people know about unions. Researchers find that many know surprisingly little. This is as true of high school students as it is of adults. When a research team at Purdue University tested 2000 high school students on their factual knowledge of labor relations, of those who took the examination over half scored 45 per cent or lower. The research I conducted in my region had similar results.

Only seven of the 120 high school students I questioned knew the number of union members in this country. The great majority said over 40 million. Several said over 60 million. The actual figure, as discussed earlier, is somewhat over 20 million.

Only nineteen students, or one in six, could explain what the AFL–CIO is and what it does.

Only half knew the difference between a local union and an international union.

Only seventeen, or about one in seven, had a clear sense of how many contract negotiations actually break down and result in strikes. Over half said one in four. Over a third said one in two. Actually only one in twenty are not settled peacefully in a typical year.

Few students could identify labor's leaders. For example, only twenty-two knew of Samuel Gompers, the father of the American labor movement. Only eleven could identify George Meany, who for many years had headed the AFL–CIO. Only twelve could identify Walter Reuther, then president of the United Automobile Workers and the nation's second most powerful labor leader. On the other hand, almost everyone questioned had heard of Jimmy Hoffa, the president of the Teamsters union who then was serving a prison term for his practices while in office. (For a description of this survey see the Preface.)

Most people get their information on unions from two sources: the press and the schools. However, union officials claim that the press does not give a true picture of labor's activities and achievements. They criticize the emphasis it places on conflicts such as deadlocks in bargaining, strikes, and disputes over racial discrimination. They complain that unions are portrayed as selfish, irresponsible organizations when in fact the overwhelming majority are as responsible as the employers with whom they deal. They point with pride to the tens of thousands of contracts they negotiate each year without strikes, to the great numbers of honest, dedicated union officials, to the political and social work unions undertake in behalf of the underprivileged, all of which they say is overlooked or downgraded by the press.

The schools also come in for criticism. Labor leaders and researchers at various universities maintain that many schools and many textbooks place too much emphasis on the turmoil that developed as workers tried to establish unions and too little on current relationships between unions and employers. Labor leaders in the South also are concerned by the lack of attention universities in that region give to labor relations. At the University of Virginia, for example, the first course on unionism ever offered at that school was introduced in 1968. Although many students welcomed the course, many businessmen did not. In fact, the Virginia Chamber of Commerce organized a statewide letter-writing campaign to abolish such instruction, but the university stood fast.

Inevitably, our ideas about unions and management also are shaped by the values, opinions, and experiences of others with whom we come in contact. The attitudes of young people, for example, frequently are influenced in part, and at least for a period, by those of their parents and their friends. As a result, those whose fathers are in management frequently tend to see things as management does. In fact, some may be far more militant about confronting unions and show less sensitivity to the problems of workers than their fathers, who must deal with the realities of life.

Dr. William H. Kaven, professor of economics at the University of Virginia, has had several experiences which bear this out. On one occasion, during a discussion of the wages workers are paid, a student argued that it was poor business to pay a man more than he is worth.

"How much do you pay him in Southside Virginia?" Dr. Kaven asked.

"Fifty cents an hour for ten hours, Sir."

"How do you know that's all he's worth?"

"Because, Sir, that's what we can get him for."

On another occasion, he invited Ernest Rice McKinney, an eighty-one-year-old Negro who had been an organizer for the Steelworkers union, to talk to his class. The conversation turned to jobs for poor blacks in Mississippi. One student contended that there were plenty of jobs available, and if the poor people in Mississippi "would only get off their backs" and go where the jobs were they would have plenty of work. He suggested Detroit.

"They have no money," Mr. McKinney said. "How will they get there?"

"Let them walk, Sir."

"But they have no money for food. What will they eat?"

"Let them hunt and fish along the way. If my grandfather could do it, they can do it." *

Young people from working class families tend to view things from quite a different perspective. They stress the need for protection against exploitation by employers. Without unions, many feel that the wages, working conditions, and job security their parents have won would be endangered and future gains would be impossible. In my study of high school students, 63 per cent of those from union families said that when they took a job they wanted to join a union. Only 30 per cent of those from nonunion families felt this way.

Of course, attitudes regarding unions and management also are shaped by events. A long strike, violence on the picket line, unfair treatment of workers, racial discrimination by a union, and criminal acts all have their impact. So do official positions labor unions and labor federations take on issues ranging from its support of public aid for education to its support of the war the United States waged in Vietnam.

THERE ARE NO BYSTANDERS

Over the long term everyone is affected by the relationship between labor and management. Whether or not we are

---

* *Labor Breakthrough in the Southern Classroom* (New York: League for Industrial Democracy, 1968).

union members, our wages, our taxes, what we pay for goods and services, the number of jobs available, even the changing nature of work are influenced by the agreements labor and management reach. So important is our stake in these contracts, some specialists urge that the public have its own representatives at the bargaining table to help shape the decisions that are made. This may yet come to pass, but for now our influence on labor relations is far more limited.

Ordinarily we rely on the government to represent our interests, but those who expect decisive action often are disappointed. With the need to balance the rights and interests of all groups affected, the government tends to move slowly. Thus, when a strike erupts or when wages and prices rise at an inflationary rate, it simply may urge restraint. Or it may develop guidelines it asks labor and management to follow in deciding on increases. Or it may provide mediators to settle a dispute or if necessary it may exert pressure to force an agreement. If a severe, deeply rooted problem becomes apparent it even may pass a law to deal with it. But all this takes time. Moreover, whether the action taken is in the public interest depends largely on how one sees things.

If members of the public wish to affect government policies, they must, of course, make themselves heard. However, this is more easily said than done. Traditionally citizens voice their opinions through letters to public officials, through their votes, and in public opinion polls. If the pressure for change is great enough, in one way or another the government eventually responds. It may increase its pressure on labor and management to take the public into account. Or in extreme cases it may impose more stringent regulations. Thus, widespread frustration over strikes was a major factor in the passage of the Taft–Hartley Act. Public concern over corruption in labor–management relations also helped assure passage of the Landrum–Griffin Act (see chapter 11).*

In some cases pressures for change are mobilized by labor or management or their allies, all of whom rely at least in part on public support. To obtain advantages for their side, such groups may seek to ban or legalize the union shop in their state, to make it more or less difficult to organize local unions, or to expand or limit management's rights or labor's rights. Or they may seek other changes that someday may affect your pocketbook or your job. Of course, whether we use our influence wisely in such situations depends on how much we know about the issues and the extent to which we are willing to place the public interest above our own interest.

---

* For a discussion of how opinions form and affect our lives, see *What Do You Think?* by Alvin Schwartz (New York: E. P. Dutton & Company, 1966).

Part Four | UNIONS AT WORK

A union has but one reason for being: to improve the lives of its members. How it defines this job and how successful it is vary with the union. But as we have seen, virtually every union sets itself at least three tasks. One is to build its membership and thereby increase its strength and effectiveness. Another is to bargain for its members over their wages, hours, and working conditions. The third is to press for the passage of laws that benefit unions and workers.

13 | Organizing the Unorganized

Unions acquire their members in a number of ways. They obtain many automatically through union shop agreements which require that the workers an employer hires join their union. In some cases they also gain members through mergers with other unions. But the most important way they grow is by organizing new locals, for only by organizing the unorganized can unionism spread. When Samuel Gompers led the labor movement he ended every speech to a union audience with the plea "Organize! Organize! Organize!" Labor leaders still regard organizing as an "unending mission." And employers still see it as an unending threat.

The year this was written international unions in the United States organized 5000 new locals in factories, offices, schools, stores, hospitals, and other work places. One result was that the unions gained 300,000 members. Another was a totally new relationship between these workers and their employers which affected not only pay and benefits, but work rules, methods of doing business, prices, profits, and other matters of importance.

There are unions that do not actively recruit members. The skilled craftsmen in the building trades are a case in point. They prefer to limit the labor supply in their occupations and thereby keep wages high. But most unions work hard at organizing. The Textile Workers Union of America, for example, spends two-thirds of its budget in this way. In the South alone, where only one textile worker in three is a union member, the union has forty full-time organizers at work. But even giant unions which have organized almost all the workers in an industry or an occupation continue to recruit members in related fields. In a recent year, for example, the United Auto Workers established 273 new local unions in companies that make parts for cars and in firms in the aerospace and farm-equipment industries.

In line with a long tradition of brotherhood, unions often help one another with their organizing efforts, sharing information, advice, and manpower, even contributing funds when needed. The AFL–CIO also is a source of help. It operates a school in Washington, D.C., where unions send their organizers for training, and has organizers of its own throughout the country to which unions may turn. It also sponsors organizing campaigns in which unions join forces in a particular area.

But labor leaders do not always behave like brothers. At times they compete for members, just as businessmen compete for customers. Thus, the American Federation of Teachers competes with the National Education Association, the Textile Workers Union competes with the United Textile Workers, and the Machinists compete with the Auto Workers. In some cases two or more unions may try to organize the same workers at the same work place, fighting one another as well as management. Or a union may "raid" a local union that was organized by a competitor and try to build support to challenge it in a new representation election. Since such competition is wasteful, labor's leaders try to curb it. Unions sign "no-raiding" agreements, and when disputes do arise the AFL–CIO provides mediators to settle them. But the competition persists.

Unions work as hard as they do at organizing for good reason. When many workers in a region are not unionized, it makes it harder to raise wages for those who are members. The larger an international union, moreover, the more weight it carries with employers and the more influence it has with lawmakers. Of course, a growing membership also means a larger income from dues with which to hire a staff and develop benefits that attract still more members.

However, organizing new locals is not as easy as it once was. An important reason is that workers have changed. Many are better educated than they were in the past. In the 1930s the vast majority of those who joined unions had not gone beyond grade school. Today most have a high school education and a growing number have one or more college degrees. At one time, moreover, a fiery speech about "the capitalistic few" and a rousing song about the downtrodden were all that were needed to tap the resentment workers felt and bring them into unions. They would sing:

> "Don't scab for the bosses,
> Don't listen to their lies,
> Us poor folks haven't got a chance,
> Unless we organize. . . ."

With no property, with no certainty their jobs would last, with their lives dominated by want, they had nothing to lose. Many of the workers unions seek today as members never have known severe deprivation. Moreover, many have the option of quitting and taking another job. In addition, many have acquired property and in a sense have become "capitalists" in their own right. Through the use of credit, they own houses, cars, and appliances they pay for month by month and year by year, financial responsibilities that have made them more conservative. When the question of organizing a union arises, and with it the possibility of a strike that will curtail a worker's income, he thinks twice about joining. And fiery speeches and songs about the downtrodden usually do not satisfy him. The laws that regulate organizing also have changed. In the 1930s they placed severe restrictions on steps an employer could take to oppose unions. Today employers have far more freedom and make effective use of it, as we shall see.

As noted earlier, about 20 million workers in the United States belong to unions or associations that behave like unions. Officials at the AFL–CIO estimate that there are another 30 million workers who could be organized. But whether they will be depends on several factors. One is whether the nation's laws encourage or discourage unionism. Another is how fairly employers treat their employees. But the most crucial is whether a worker feels he can deal best with his problems by joining a union or by standing alone, and this depends on the unions as well as on the employers.

On almost any day there are several thousand union organizers at work. Most are former union members whose natu-
ral talents as salesmen, speakers, administrators, and amateur
psychologists enable them to earn their living in this unusual
trade. There are organizers who are more concerned with
bringing in dues-paying members than with helping workers
solve their problems. But a great many have an idealistic interest in seeing unionism spread. It could not be otherwise,
for the work of the organizer is hard, rough, tiresome, frequently secretive, often unpleasant, often disappointing, and
at times dangerous. Moreover, the hours are long, a great
deal of time is spent on the road, and the pay is not exactly
generous.

The raw material of the organizer's trade is discontent.
Wherever it exists so does the possibility that a union can be
formed. The organizer's job is to find dissatisfaction, bring it
to the surface, nurture it, demonstrate that a union can solve
the problem, then help the workers involved form a local
union of their own. Of course, dissatisfaction does not exist
everywhere, but there is more than enough to keep union organizers busy. There are times, in fact, when workers are so
troubled by conditions on the job they seek out a union and
ask for help, as a North Carolina mill hand did in this letter
to the Textile Workers union:

"Won't you please see if you can get the union here for
us," he wrote. "We are fed up with dirty treatment. The
workers are scared to say so . . . but I think most of us want
the union. . . . They are working us just like slaves and
nothing matters to them except [making] more money. . . .
I can't sign my name to this 'cause I'd be fired."

Sometimes the request comes over the telephone. When
an electronics company in Aurora, New York, eliminated its
annual Christmas bonus, a group of women at the plant re-

garded it as the last straw. Their pay averaged $1.35 an hour and without the bonus they faced serious financial problems. As they saw it, the only solution was to call the regional office of the United Auto Workers in nearby Buffalo and ask for help. The result, after several months, was UAW Local 1416. But when an organizer has no contacts, his first task is to make some.

Some organizers do this by distributing leaflets to workers as they enter or leave a plant or an office, a procedure they call leafleting. The folder usually includes a coupon a worker can use to request more information about forming a union. One of the many folders the Textile Workers union distributes carries a drawing of a fat, bald businessman surrounded by money bags labeled "Advertising," "Plant Expansion," "New Machinery," and "Public Relations." "MONEY FOR EVERYTHING . . . BUT YOU!" the headline declares. The union then concentrates on those work places that yield the largest number of coupons.

However, other organizers prefer to keep management unaware of their activities as long as possible. They determine which restaurants, taverns, and bowling alleys workers frequent, then visit these places in an effort to meet them and determine what their interest in unionism may be. A few even check the license plate numbers of cars in company parking lots, determine from the government who own the cars, then either write the owners or follow them home.

If an organizer finds a person who wants to form a union, he then may ask him to bring four or five other workers who feel as he does to a meeting. If all goes well he then arranges a second, larger meeting. At these sessions he answers scores of questions. But he also seeks answers to questions of his own. For example: what actually is troubling these people? Do their complaints reflect important problems or are they rooted in personality conflicts? How loyal are they to their employer? Despite protective laws, would they lose their jobs if they joined a union? Would they support a strike if the need for one arose? Would their employer fight the formation of a union? Would he have the support of the police, the clergy, and business leaders in such a fight?

In every case the answers are crucial, for the workers who cast their lot with a union may risk a strike, a loss of income, and in some cases their jobs. The union, in turn, may risk its reputation and its funds. Some organizing campaigns involve but one union representative and a few thousand dollars, but there are others that involve many organizers and large sums for salaries, motel bills, literature, and other expenses. In fact, there are unions that have spent $100,000 on a single campaign. If initially the conditions do not seem right, an organizer will move on and try again in a year or two. But if there is a reasonable chance of success, he may make the effort.

MOVING AHEAD

In some cases a union may try to organize all the employees in a work place. In others it may concentrate on those in a particular occupation, such as the production workers in a factory or the teachers in a school system. In every case its goal is to recruit enough members so that it can serve as their bargaining agent. As noted earlier, a government may conduct a representation election to determine whether a majority of workers want the union (see chapter 11). If an election is not required, as is the case in many states, the union and the employer must settle the matter on their own, which frequently means a strike.

Once the decision to move ahead has been made, the first

step is to form an organizing committee of workers to serve
as the nucleus of a new local. Selecting its members is the
most critical step in the entire process, for a committee
whose members are respected by other workers can mean
the difference between failure and success. The committee's
job is to build the union. Before and after work, at coffee
breaks, in the lunchroom, in the locker room, its members try
to sell other workers on joining. They come armed with
facts, figures, and descriptions of improvements formation of
a union might mean. They also come armed with authorization cards. When a worker signs such a card he gives the
union the right to bargain for him with his employer. Each
day the committee meets with the organizer to review which
workers are joining, which are not, and what strategy to follow.

WHICH SIDE ARE YOU ON?

Some of the workers the committee approaches are eager to
join. They may have a serious grievance they cannot resolve
themselves and see a union as the only answer. They may
have belonged to a union elsewhere and found it worthwhile. They may have a tradition of unionism in their family.
They may join because they want to be with the group and
are willing to follow its lead. Or they may get tired of the
constant pressure to join. As one worker put it, "They approach you again and again, keep after you, hound you, and
finally you join to get them off your back." Or they may fear,
correctly or incorrectly, that if they do not join, their work
will be sabotaged or they will be beaten (see chapter 8).

Others do not know what to do about joining. They may
be concerned about their jobs and their chances for promotion. They may have deep respect for their boss and wonder how in good conscience they can become part of a group

Authorization for Representation Under the National Labor Relations Act

I, the undersigned, employee of

_____
Company

_____
Address of Company

authorize the International Chemical Workers Union to represent me in all matters relating to collective bargaining. This authorization card may be used for a card check or for any other method to achieve recognition or certification of the ICWU as the collective bargaining agent, and supersedes any similar authority previously given to any person or organization.

My Job Is_____Shift_____

Area_____Home Phone_____

My Address_____City_____

My Signature_____Date_____

Witness to Signature_____Date_____

*An authorization card which gives a
union the right to bargain for a worker.*

that opposes him. They may be concerned about the union itself, about the degree of freedom they will have or about the amount of coercion to which they will be subjected. In such cases members of the organizing committee may visit a worker at his home to convince him that his doubts are unfounded, but they do not always succeed.

Even if the organizer and his committee have been operating secretly, there comes a time when this no longer is practical. To reach the many workers whose support they need, at some point they must rely on posters, newspaper ads, letters, radio commercials, and other communications to state their case.

Within a few weeks an organizer will know where he stands. If authorization cards are not being signed in large numbers, he will abandon his effort for the time being and move on. But if the majority the union seeks signs up, he will take a different course. He may show the employer the authorization cards and ask him to recognize the union. If the employer is convinced that a majority want the union, he may agree. But if he feels his employees can be won back or that their union can be destroyed, he may not. If a labor law does not apply and an election is not required, the union may respond by striking. But if there is a law, the employer may insist on an election and mount a counterattack.

THE ELECTION AT LOUDON, TENNESSEE

The notice from the National Labor Relations Board arrived September 16. It announced that the International Chemical Workers Union claimed the right to bargain for 361 production and maintenance workers at the food-products plant in town and had asked for a representation election. As required by law, the union had submitted authorization cards signed by at least 30 per cent of the workers. The NLRB now wanted to schedule a meeting to discuss the proposed election. It was the third attempt by the union to organize the workers at Loudon. The officials who managed the plant for a large corporation, which asked that its name not be used in this account, were aware of the effort, but up to that point had done nothing to resist.

September 20: The company posted a notice throughout the plant announcing the union's latest move. "In our opinion," it read, "the majority of people here believe that representation by outsiders is unnecessary. . . ."

September 21: The NLRB scheduled a meeting for September 28 at the Loudon County Courthouse for representatives of the company and the union. An election could be held within thirty days if the company agreed that the union was entitled to an election and both agreed on who was eligible to vote. Otherwise, a formal hearing would be needed and the election would be delayed.

September 28: The company agreed to an election within

thirty days. Voting would be by secret ballot under government supervision. It would take place October 13 in the
plant conference room. The day shift would vote from 7 A.M.
to 9 A.M., the night shift from 11 P.M. to 1 A.M. The company
posted this information throughout the plant. Then the plant
manager wrote to each employee at his home pointing out
that the company would campaign actively against the union
"to keep our relationships on a direct person to person
basis." It was the first of several letters he would send them.

September 29: The plant's supervisors were given guidelines to use in the company's campaign against the union.
They could freely argue against the union in discussions
with employees, they were told, but it was against the law to
ask an employee whether he supported the union, to
threaten reprisals, or promise rewards. Instead they were in-
structed to make several points, including the following:

> We do not believe that any union can accomplish any
> good in this plant. They are too far away from the actual
> members. They are run for the benefit of the union officers
> and not the rank and file. . . .
>
> Unions have forced up wage rates. In fact, in many indus-
> tries wages have been forced out of line so that foreign com-
> petition can hurt U.S. employment. . . .
>
> Unions create a laboring class and try to keep members
> from leaving the ranks. . . .
>
> Our wages are among the highest in this area. . . . We
> have good working conditions. . . . [You] do not have to
> pay . . . dues . . . for benefits that can be had without
> cost. . . .
>
> Unions can make all kinds of promises. They cannot guar-
> antee anything. . . .

October 1: The NLRB sent the company eighteen copies

A flyer the managers of a plant in Loudon, Tennessee, used to fight an organizing effort.

of an official Notice of Election it had to post on bulletin boards throughout the plant.

October 2: The company mailed a flyer to each employee urging that he vote against the union when the election was held. One side carried the following message:

"Many union professionals try to mislead employees into believing that union contracts provide job security. They do not! Only a successful and progressive business with all of us working as a team can give you real job security!"

On the other side a cartoon depicted employees laughing at a union organizer.

October 4: The company mailed each employee a postal card which announced that he could hear a recorded message from the plant manager if he dialed a particular telephone number. If he wished he could make anonymous comments which would be recorded. Each day until the election there would be a new message. The company also distributed the first of several handbills stressing the disadvantages of union membership.

October 6: The first telephone message was played:

How are you? This is Ray Birkholz.

Have you ever wondered why unions keep knocking on your door, hoping to get into the Loudon plant? It costs plenty of money for a union to run an organizing campaign. . . . But big as the organizing costs are, they are peanuts compared with the dues employees would pay if the union got in the plant here. You and your fellow employees at the plant represent $20,000 a year to the union in dues. . . .

If you don't want to pay union dues—if you don't want to pay salaries and expenses for union organizers—all you have to do is vote NO in the election next Wednesday.

October 7: To encourage antiunion sentiment in the community, the company ran an advertisement in the local news-

, "Some of the Reasons Why We Do Not Need It scheduled a series of meetings at which the manager would speak to employees about the union campaign. In accordance with the law, attendance was voluntary.

October 8: The plant manager addressed the first of nine employee meetings, including one at midnight for members of the night shift.

"We have problems here, as does any large organization of human beings," he declared. "But a union won't solve these problems. . . . [they] would only multiply and fester. You and management can get better results by continuing to work together with understanding and friendship. . . ."

October 11: The company reminded its supervisors that the law banned electioneering in the twenty-four hours preceding the election. Meanwhile, the plant manager wrote to the employees once more. "You must decide," he told them, "whether the Loudon plant will continue to be a friendly place to work, a place where employees earn good wages, good working conditions, and good benefit plans; *or* a place which will be in an uproar as the union sets one group of employees against another group, a place where employees will live under the threat of strikes. The choice is up to you."

Of course, in this period the union also was at work, relying on many of the techniques described earlier. In the final days its organizer and its organizing committee concentrated on those employees who had not yet made up their minds. In the final hours they worked to get those who wanted a union to the polls.

When the employees at Loudon cast their ballots on October 13, 164 voted for the union to serve as their collective bargaining agent. But 187 voted against the union. The outcome was a narrow victory for management, but the number

The type of ballot the National Labor Relations Board uses in union representation elections.

of votes for the union—46 per cent of those cast—spoke clearly of unrest. Under the law the union could try again after a year had elapsed. Whether it would succeed, however, would depend largely on the success the company had in dealing with discontent.

"IF YOU MESS WITH THE UNION, YOU GOT TROUBLE"

Many employers respond to an organizing campaign just as did the managers in Loudon. They vigorously oppose unionism, yet they stay within the limits of the law. However, there are some who are not concerned merely with winning an election. They want to crush the fledgling union, punish those workers who joined, and make sure there are no further attempts to organize, no matter what tactics are necessary. A suprising number of employers have such objectives. But it is in the smaller cities and towns, particularly in the South, the Middle West, and the Southwest, where the largest number are found and where resistance to unionism is strongest.

Invariably these communities are conservative places where change comes slowly, outsiders and new ideas are suspect, and fear of racial integration, a process most unions foster, is strong. Moreover, most are not prosperous, relying for jobs and income on but one or two large companies. Many such employers for years have enjoyed the advantages of a low wage scale, low taxes, and freedom from unions. In fact, a sizable number moved from the North to escape high taxes, high wages, and strong unions. Since World War II much of the textile industry has relocated for these reasons. Since the payroll such firms bring with them means increased prosperity for a community, its leaders work hard to attract them, and once they arrive do everything they can to keep their owners happy.

"When you hit such a town," an organizer for the United Auto Workers observed, "you'd better walk on cotton because they are watching you every minute." At least one Chamber of Commerce tries to do just that, issuing periodic reports on the current whereabouts of union organizers. An organizer in a hostile town also may encounter problems that were common before Congress recognized the right to form a union and bargain collectively with an employer. He may have trouble finding a room in which to sleep or a hall in which to hold a meeting. He may be tailed by police who prevent him from distributing leaflets and harass him in

A union organizer after his arrest in Chattanooga, Tennessee.

other ways. He may even be attacked physically by supervisors or by workers who fear he may cause trouble. Some organizers have had leaflets knocked from their hands and have been pelted with tomatoes and squirted with fire extinguishers. Still others have been beaten and run out of town. However, employers in such towns worry more about workers who might consider a union than about organizers. As one mill hand explained, "If you mess with the union, you got trouble." To avoid "troublemakers" some employers closely question job applicants about unionism before hiring them. Others rely on a blacklist of men and women in their area who are known to favor unionism. If an organizer begins to sign up their workers, moreover, there are several steps they may take. Some may hold compulsory meetings for their employees at which they warn of layoffs and wage cuts if a union is formed, and attack the union's organizers as

"Communists," "crooks," and in some areas as "nigger-lovers" and "New York Jews." They may try to discover which employees are joining the union, then pressure them to withdraw, and, if they fail to do so, fire them. They also may enlist the help of the town fathers. The newspaper editor may write editorials warning of what strikes will do to the local economy. Merchants and bankers may try to influence workers who owe them money. Even ministers may join in with attacks on the union from their pulpits.

Many of these tactics are unfair labor practices that violate Federal or state laws. However, some employers use them anyway, for the penalties are minor when measured against the results. Thus, firing the members of an organizing committee may stop an organizing campaign in its tracks. If a company is found guilty by the NLRB, usually all it must do is rehire the workers if they want their jobs back, pay them what they would have earned, and post a notice on its bulletin boards promising not to violate the law again in this way. Although the back pay involved may be sizable, the savings from operating without a union usually are far greater.

Breaking the law may undermine an organizing effort in another way. Months may elapse before the employer is found guilty. If he appeals the decision from court to court, as is his privilege, far more time is involved. Meanwhile the fledgling union cannot press for recognition until the matter is settled. And the longer it waits the less chance it has of surviving, even if the company finally is found guilty. Unions have fought for years to strengthen the penalties involved and eliminate other loopholes in the law, but without success.

One of the most dramatic cases of this kind involved 550 workers in a textile mill in Darlington, South Carolina, and the mill's owners, Deering Millikin & Company, a major firm with operations throughout the South. During an organizing campaign, the company declared it would close the mill if it had to deal with a union. When its employees voted to have the Textile Workers Union represent them, the company carried out its threat. The following month it closed the mill. Two months later it sold the looms and the other equipment. Since the mill was the only large employer in town, many of its employees had trouble finding work and were reduced to picking cotton and baby-sitting. Some finally found jobs in distant communities and others moved away.

The union, meanwhile, set up a relief kitchen, raised money for the destitute, and undertook a legal fight to correct the situation. When the National Labor Relations Board found the company guilty of unfair labor practices, the firm appealed to court after court. Only when the United States Supreme Court rejected its final appeal did the company pay the workers the tens of thousands of dollars they had lost in pay and benefits and offer to rehire them at its other mills. But the company's legal maneuvers had consumed thirteen years. As one of its former workers observed, "Mr. Millikin, he done us a damned shameful deed."

Despite many obstacles unions do manage to win elections and establish bargaining relationships in such areas. During 1969 and 1970, the Textile Workers organized over 7000 mill hands in the South. But it took far more patience, determination, courage, and money than ordinarily is the case.

14 | Collective Bargaining: The Issues

When Samuel Gompers was asked many years ago what labor wanted, he replied, "More!" Today union members still want more. Like all of us, they want more income, more security, and more opportunity to make something of their lives. However, management also wants "more." It wants higher profits, lower costs, more control over its work force, and more freedom to operate as it sees fit. Inevitably, the objectives of one side conflict with those of the other.

MORE MONEY

Labor's demand for more money is the one with which it has had the most success. One study found that workers in unionized factories earned 18 per cent more than those in non-union shops. Although unions do not always achieve their bargaining goals, usually most win some of what they seek. Typically this includes an increase in basic pay, but often it also involves a variety of other improvements. Through his union's efforts, a worker may earn extra pay for overtime, night work, or hazardous work. He may be eligible for cost-of-living increases, profit-sharing payments, and Christmas bonuses. If he is laid off during a slack period, his employer may have to pay him part of the income he loses. He also is likely to receive paid insurance, vacations, and other fringe benefits discussed later.

There are times, however, when union members willingly forego a pay increase. This was the case in Los Angeles when teachers gave up a raise so that classes could be reduced in size and reading programs could be improved. This also was the case in Lancaster, Pennsylvania, where 1200 members of a watch workers union voted to cut their wages by 10 per cent for half a year to help the Hamilton Watch Company out of a financial bind. The decision meant a loss in pay of up to eighteen dollars a week for the workers and their families.

But ordinarily almost every negotiation includes a demand for more income. In some situations, the goal is merely a decent standard of living, which was the case with the hospital workers in New York when they sought to increase the thirty-two dollars they were being paid for a forty-four-hour week (see chapter 8). In other cases, unions argue that their members are entitled to a raise because they have become more experienced and more productive, because the employer is making a larger profit in which workers should share, or because inflation is cutting their purchasing power and they need more money to meet the rising cost of living.

In fact, it is during periods of severe inflation that the pressures for wage increases are greatest. When this was written inflation was rampant. In the three years that had just passed, raises totaling as much as thirty dollars a week had been canceled by rising prices. In turn, workers demanded still larger increases. That year electrical workers, merchant seamen, airline employees, policemen, teachers, and truck drivers won increases of 10 to 20 per cent, and others were even more successful. But almost every raise sent the cost of living still higher. When, for example, the men who delivered milk in New York won a twenty-seven-dollar a week increase, the price of milk rose by as much as five cents a quart or seventy dollars a year for a family with two children. When the city's transit workers won a major raise that year, bus and subway fares immediately rose ten cents, or fifty dollars a year more for the average worker.

Of course, each side blames the other for pushing prices higher. Employers say that the raises unions "force" on them are not realistic, that frequently their employees do not increase their production of goods or services enough to cover the costs involved. As a result, they explain, they raise prices to make up the difference. However, union leaders contend that the profits employers make often are more than enough to absorb higher wages without raising prices. Whoever is responsible for this wage–price spiral, and often both sides share the blame, the result feeds inflation. But when the Federal government urges that labor and management use restraint in increasing costs, they tend to resist. Both oppose outside interference in their affairs. However, growing numbers of the public who suffer the consequences do not share this feeling.

Under mounting pressure to bring inflation to a halt, in 1971 the government finally took steps to stop the wage-price spiral. President Richard Nixon established a pay board to set standards for noninflationary wage increases and to recommend legal action against violations. As its members he appointed representatives of labor, management, and the public. To keep prices in line he appointed a price commission solely from the public sector. Both labor and management agreed to cooperate in the experiment. But the extent to which it would succeed depended in large part on the sacrifices they were willing to make.

MORE BENEFITS

Unions also place heavy emphasis in their negotiations on insurance, pensions, and other fringe benefits they believe an employer should provide. They do so in line with a European tradition that an employer has a social as well as an economic responsibility to his employees, that his relationship with them does not stop at the end of a work day or a career. In Europe the government, frequently under pressure from unions, insists that employers meet this responsibility. In Belgium, for example, the law requires that employers pay the cost of "sick insurance" for their employees. In Italy an employer must provide sixteen paid holidays a year. In Sweden he must grant an annual four-week vacation (see chapter 19). In the United States, these matters depend largely on private negotiation between an employer and a union, with the result that benefits vary from work place to work place.

There are employers who feel a strong responsibility to

provide fringe benefits, but there are many more who go along largely for selfish reasons. A good benefits program enables them to compete more effectively for new workers and keep those they have from moving to other jobs. It also forestalls any move to broaden our national system of benefits, to which employers must contribute but which do not yield any competitive advantage if all citizens are affected.

Despite their great impact on our lives, fringe benefits actually are a recent development in the United States. It was not until World War II that most employers began such programs. In that period the government tightly controlled wages to keep inflation in rein. To keep the workers they had satisfied and to attract others they badly needed, employers agreed to bargain over fringe benefits, with results that few anticipated.

In the years that followed, fringe benefits became a major means of compensation in this country. Some employers are more generous than others, but as a group they now spend over $100 billion a year on "fringes," or about twenty cents of every dollar they spend on wages. These expenditures provide tens of millions of families with important protection against the pitfalls of life. They also provide time and money for increased leisure. They have become so important that many workers change jobs not only for better wages, but for better health insurance or a more generous retirement plan. They have become so costly they often require far more time at the bargaining table than do wage discussions. They have become so complex that, in their negotiations, labor and management frequently must rely on insurance experts, pension specialists, accountants, and computers. When the Metropolitan Transit Authority in New York negotiated a contract with the Transport Workers Union, for example, pension experts developed 175 different approaches to retirement pay.

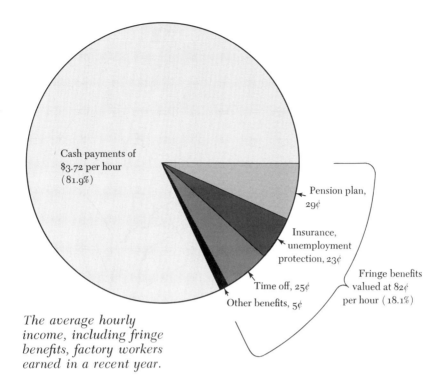

Cash payments of
$3.72 per hour
(81.9%)

Pension plan,
29¢

Insurance,
unemployment
protection, 23¢

Time off, 25¢

Other benefits, 5¢

Fringe benefits
valued at 82¢
per hour (18.1%)

*The average hourly
income, including fringe
benefits, factory workers
earned in a recent year.*

The benefits unions now seek or employers voluntarily grant extend well beyond those considered realistic a generation ago. Not all unionized workers have them, but a growing number do. Some health-insurance programs provide protection against medical catastrophes which otherwise could bankrupt a family. In addition, they cover dental care, psychiatric care, and the cost of medicines and eye glasses. The Major League Baseball Players Association also has an agreement which covers the costly surgery baseball pitchers sometimes need to correct "sore" arms. Most union members also are covered by life insurance for which their employers pay, and a few, whose numbers may increase, are even protected against the cost of accidents in driving to and from work. Pensions are another benefit of great importance. They provide almost 50 million persons with retirement funds to supplement Social Security payments. Moreover, many workers now may retire when they are fifty-five or younger, instead of at sixty-five, as has been traditional, and receive at least part of their pension.

In addition, unions are slowly winning more leisure time for their members. In some occupations workers have ten paid holidays a year and vacations that range up to a month or five weeks. In the steel, can, and aluminum industries, workers with long service also are entitled to a thirteen-week vacation once every five years, along with their regular vacation. A growing number of teachers are eligible for a one-year leave of absence at half pay. There also are unions that have won vacation bonuses for their members so that they will have the money to enjoy the time off they receive.

Unions also are making gains which might seem to have little to do with an employer, but are good examples of the ever-changing boundaries of collective bargaining. Under one agreement, men's clothing manufacturers now pay part of the college tuition each year for children of long-term workers. Under another, as noted earlier, they set up free day-care centers near their factories so that working mothers have a decent place to leave their children.

The agreement the Seafarers International Union negotiates with shipowners provides that each seaman be supplied with the following items:

"A suitable number of blankets.

"Bedding consisting of two white sheets, one bedspread, and two white pillow slips, which must be changed weekly.

"One face towel and one bath towel which shall be changed twice weekly. . . .

"One cake of standard face soap . . . with each towel change.

"One box of matches each day.

"Suitable mattresses and pillows. . . ."

Other clauses deal with the number of men per room (the goal is a private room for each seaman), the furnishings and ventilation, the availability of washing machines, refrigerators, and TV sets, food (on a foreign voyage, for example, there must be enough canned milk so that each man may have a pint a day), and scores of other matters that affect the daily lives of the crew. Although few unions find it necessary to go into such detail, virtually every one bargains over the conditions under which its members work.

With migrant farm workers the need for a portable toilet in the fields or a comfortable dormitory in which to spend the night may be a matter for the bargaining table. With actors, it may be a clean, private room in which to change their clothes. With office workers, it may be good lighting. With miners, it may be safety. With teachers it may be the size of their classes, the quality of their textbooks, or the procedures to deal with disruptive students.

The amount of time a worker must spend on the job also is subject to negotiation. In 1900 the average was about fifty-six hours a week. Today it is between thirty-five and forty hours, and every union wants to reduce this further. Some have as their goal a four-day, twenty-eight-hour week. When a union discusses time, however, other questions also may be involved. In textile mills, the issue may be time to eat lunch, for often a worker must eat when he can at his loom. In schools where teachers must supervise a playground at lunch, a duty-free lunch period may be the issue. With musicians, it may be rehearsal time; with stagehands, curtain time; with welfare workers, the number of meetings they must attend after working hours.

Not too many years ago time for a coffee break was a major source of conflict at the bargaining table. But today employees everywhere, including those who do not belong to unions, regard a break as an inalienable right. For ten minutes, or more, each morning and each afternoon, they stop work to relax over coffee. It may not seem like anything to argue about, but it does involve eighty hours a year or two full weeks with pay for each worker. However, as the unions successfully argued, a break in the daily routine does increase efficiency and morale.

MORE SECURITY, MORE FREEDOM

To make his life more secure, to live as well as he can, a worker also wants to be sure of his job. To operate his business efficiently, to make as large a profit as he can, his employer wants to make decisions as he sees fit. Both have reasonable goals, but inevitably their objectives clash. For example: Does an employer have the right to fire whomever he wishes, for whatever reason he chooses? Can he promote anyone he wants? Can he install equipment that costs a worker his job? Can he move his plant to another location?

For most of our history an employer freely made such decisions on his own. If he had to fire a worker because he no longer was needed or if he wished for any reason to move his operation, he did so as a matter of course. But when in 1935 the law required that employers and unions bargain over conditions of employment things began to change. Through the give and take of bargaining, through decisions by the National Labor Relations Board when the two sides cannot agree, the unions gradually have acquired a voice in matters that management once regarded as its exclusive domain.

As a result workers have won a degree of security in their jobs they did not know in earlier days. In the process employers have lost part of the freedom to manage as they see fit. Union leaders regard this as a step forward, but members of management do not. As one argued, "When our ability to increase efficiency and productivity are limited, not only does the business suffer, so does job security." Just how much freedom management needs to function efficiently is a controversial question. How much job security a worker needs is another. Since there are no answers that apply in every case, these questions are a continuing source of conflict.

If a worker has a reasonably strong union he is likely to have at least two types of job protection. One is a grievance system, described in chapter 7, which assures, among other things, that he cannot be fired without just cause. If a worker feels he has been treated unfairly, his union and employer try to settle the issue. If they cannot, an arbitrator does. The other is a seniority system which provides a defense against favoritism by an employer in promotions and layoffs. Under this arrangement workers with the longest service are the first to be considered for promotion and the last to be laid off if the work force must be reduced.

Union contracts also may contain a number of other protections. In some cases an employer agrees to consult a union before changing the nature of a job, establishing a new job, or hiring outside firms to handle work his employees now do, thereby reducing his costs. In contracts that garment unions negotiate, clothing manufacturers also agree not to move their factories without written consent of the union. The objective is to discourage "runaways," employers who try to escape the high cost of unionism by dismantling their equipment during a weekend and slipping away to a more congenial location, often in the South. When the union involved catches up with such an employer and sues him, a court frequently will require that he reopen at his old location and rehire his old workers.

But most employers strenuously resist as many such commitments as they can. Many are willing to bargain over the *effects* of their decisions to move a plant or modernize it or subcontract work. But they insist that the decision to take such a step is one that they alone can make since they are responsible for the well-being of the organization. However, the unions do not always agree with this reasoning and at times they have the government on their side.

Automation. For many workers the major threat to job security is automation. Each year tens of thousands of men and women lose their jobs to machines which do their work more efficiently and more cheaply than they can. When English workingmen were confronted with such a situation early in the nineteenth century, they systematically wrecked the machines. Although today's workers may have similar feelings, they rely on unions rather than sledgehammers to protect them from change.

For many years unions vigorously resisted automation. In some cases their members would not use newly developed labor-saving equipment or techniques out of fear they would reduce the number of jobs available. Thus, painters refused to use spray guns, printers refused to use automatic type-setting equipment, and construction workers would not use prefabricated materials. Even when such techniques finally were adopted, a union might pressure an employer into "featherbedding" or "make-work" arrangements, under which employees who no longer were needed were kept on. Railroad firemen, for example, continued to occupy a place in the locomotive cabs even though the steam engines they once helped operate long since had been replaced by diesel engines which did not require their skills. The same was true of flight engineers who were essential to the operation of propeller-driven airliners. When jets were introduced and

Members of the United Automobile Workers protest the growing use of automation by the General Motors Corporation.

the engineers no longer were needed, they continued to occupy a place in the cabin. One of the most degrading make-work arrangements in effect when this was written involved linotype operators for newspapers. When advertisements arrived at the newspaper in plate form ready to reproduce, the operators still set type for the ad even though the type was not needed. When they finished, they pulled a proof, made corrections, then dumped the type in a "hot box" and melted it down. They called such work "deadhorse," for it made them feel worthless. But they did it anyway for it helped protect their jobs.

There are few unions, however, that continue to resist automation. Most labor leaders reason that it is inevitable, that the best they can do is delay it. If a company must reduce its work force most unions now see their job as cushioning the impact. In some cases an employer agrees not to fire anyone, but simply not to replace workers when they resign or retire. At times an employer initiates such an approach on his own. At the Kaiser Steel plant in Fontana, California, such workers also share in the savings the new equipment produces. Other firms have transferred workers to locations where jobs are plentiful, retrained them for new jobs, or spread the work through shorter work weeks or longer vacations. Such arrangements have been made in all the basic industries. When none of this is possible, workers may be given several months to find other jobs. But, of course, there is no guarantee that they will.

There were many workers who did not have the kinds of benefits and protections described in this chapter when this book was published. In the textile mills and sawmills in the South, workers typically were given two paid holidays and a week's vacation every year. Moreover, they had no sick leave, little or no insurance, and were laid off, fired, or promoted at the whim of their employer. In addition, their salaries were as much as 30 per cent below the national average. The situation was no different in many nursing homes, restaurants, taverns, stores, offices, factories, canneries, and government agencies. It also was the case in agricultural jobs. What was surprising about such conditions was that in some cases they existed where workers had formed unions, but their unions either did not have the strength to achieve change or were not meeting their responsibilities.

15 | Collective Bargaining: Haggle and Bluff

There was a time when an employer had absolute control over the jobs he provided. He decided what the wages, hours, and working conditions would be and who would be hired, promoted, and fired. As he saw it, this was only right, for after all it was *his* business. Many employers continue to feel this way, but far fewer have the freedom they once had. A vast number now share control of the job with labor unions through contracts the two sides negotiate.

There are over 150,000 such agreements which together directly affect over 20 million workers. Since many nonunion employers use these agreements as guidelines, millions of other workers also are influenced. And, as we have seen, so are prices, taxes, and the health of the economy. Each year more than 60,000 of these contracts must be renegotiated. It is the most important job that labor unions perform.

On almost any day hundreds of negotiators are at work. On one side of a bargaining table sit an employer and his advisors. On the other side are the union officials the employees have chosen to represent them. Because workers bargain through a union rather than as individuals, the process is called collective bargaining. Although it dates to the early days of unionism, only in modern times, through the passage of the Wagner Act, did collective bargaining become a major force in the economy and an essential part of the free enterprise system.

In the United States collective bargaining typically involves negotiators for a small business and a local union representing but a few hundred workers. However, negotiators also may represent an association of small employers and a group of local unions. Or they may speak for a giant corporation like General Motors and a giant international union like the United Auto Workers. When these organizations bargain, two sets of negotiations take place. At each plant the local manager and the local union try to solve problems regarding local working conditions. Meanwhile, top-level officials deal with wages, benefits, and other economic matters that affect all the workers in the company. Bargaining also may involve an entire industry. Every three years, for example, the presidents of the nation's largest steel companies bargain as one with the United Steelworkers of America. Their decisions affect the income and the future of 400,000 workers and their families.

Over the course of a year a major company may negotiate

separate agreements with several international unions, each of which represents but a part of its work force. But increasingly these unions coordinate their demands and bargain and strike together. In the strike against the General Electric Company described in chapter 1, fourteen international unions pooled their efforts. Labor officials call this tactic coordinated bargaining. Some companies have grown so large, they say, no single union, no matter what its size, has the power to deal with them on an equal basis. The companies have fought coordinated bargaining in the courts, but thus far to no avail.

Millions of government employees also rely on collective bargaining. But there are important differences between bargaining in the private sector and bargaining in the public sector. In the private sector a vast majority of workers have a legal right to bargain through a union. But in the public sector there are states where only employees of local governments have this right. And there are others where no government employees do. In the private sector workers bargain over wages and working conditions. But in the public sector Federal and state employees usually cannot bargain over wages. When they want a raise their unions must lobby for it in Congress or a state legislature. When negotiations in the private sector break down workers may be forced to strike to gain their demands. In the public sector few workers have this right, which leaves the final decisions on a contract in the hands of their employers. But some government workers strike anyway, which complicates things even more. (In Pennsylvania and Hawaii government employees may strike under certain conditions [see chapter 17].)

No matter who is involved, however, the contracts that result from collective bargaining are crucial documents. In some cases they are only a few pages in length. In others

FIRST PARAGRAPHS OF A
LABOR–MANAGEMENT CONTRACT

---

1. PARTIES TO THE AGREEMENT

The agreement is made by and between the ROLLER BEARING COMPANY OF AMERICA, a New Jersey Corporation, with its principal office and place of business in West Trenton, New Jersey (hereinafter referred to as the "Company" or the "Employer") and the INTERNATIONAL UNION U.A.W.A. and its Local 502 (hereinafter referred to as the "Union").

WITNESSETH:

In consideration of the mutual promises to be performed by the parties hereto, and each intending to be legally bound thereby, it is mutually agreed as follows:

2. UNION RECOGNITION

The Company recognizes the Union as the exclusive collective bargaining agent for all the Company's production and maintenance employees at its plant in West Trenton, New Jersey, in respect to rates of pay, wages, hours of employment and other conditions of employment, excluding, however, office employees, supervisors, plant protection employees, matrons, cribmen, laboratory employees and time study men, pursuant and subject to the provisions of the Labor-Management Relations Act—1947 and amendments thereto.

3. UNION SECURITY

1. All present employees shall be required, as a condition of employment to become and remain members in good standing of the Union on and after the thirtieth (30th) day

---

they are as long as this book. But in every case they affect the future in countless ways.

THE GROUND RULES

To make sense of a contract negotiation it is essential to understand the ground rules. There are three of particular importance:

(1) A contract is arrived at through compromise by both sides.

(2) Agreement on a new contract must be reached before a particular date—or deadline—on which the existing contract expires. Ordinarily a contract applies for two or three years.

(3) If the two sides fail to reach agreement by the deadline, workers in the private sector may strike for gains they could not win through bargaining. As noted earlier, many government workers also strike, even though they break the law in doing so.

The ground rule regarding strikes is the most important, for without the threat of a strike there would be no need for management to take labor's demands seriously and collective bargaining would be meaningless.

AT THE BARGAINING TABLE

Negotiations over a new contract ordinarily begin two or three months before an existing contract expires. In some cases the two sides bargain in a conference room management provides. In others they move to neutral ground in a motel or a hotel. If major organizations are involved, they may move in large staffs, office equipment, and mountains of background information. Of course, each side also comes armed with a set of demands which reflect many influences: problems on the job, the cost of living, the state of the business, the results of negotiations elsewhere, and, above all, the degree of economic strength each possesses.

At the outset a spokesman for each side summarizes what it seeks. Then usually the negotiators meet several times each week to discuss the demands in detail. But these discussions involve far more than weighing the arguments involved. Initially each side uses these meetings to learn as best it can where the other stands: which of its demands are important, what it might concede, how far it might be willing to go. Both insist again and again that they want to be fair and reasonable. But both also want the best settlement they can get, for the stakes are high and, as a result, often neither is fair or reasonable.

The process of bargaining involves haggling and bluffing. In the ancient tradition of the market place, each side tries to conceal its motives while probing for those of its opponent. To learn how far management would be willing to go on the question of a wage increase, for example, a union might make an outrageously high demand. To get a sense of what the union might accept, management might counter with an offer that is outrageously low. When the Transit Workers Union in New York demanded a wage package of $259 million, the transit officials called it "incredible." When in turn they offered $84 million, the union's leaders called it "totally inadequate." Both were right. But having defined the limits of the dispute, they then could work toward a compromise.

As time slips by the pace of negotiations inevitably quickens. Instead of meeting two or three times a week, the negotiators now may meet every day, often working far into the night to achieve a compromise. But the road they travel is rarely a smooth one. Thus, a negotiator may shout and pound the table, resort to name calling, or stalk out of the bargaining session and take his team with him and not return for days. If the two sides reach a deadlock and management refuses to compromise, the union may take a strike vote among its members. If it is the union that refuses to give ground, management may threaten to close down its operations and "lock out" the workers until it wins its point. Of course, whether these threats are serious or idle remains to be seen.

In some cases one side or both may carry the struggle beyond the conference room. They may issue bulletins to the workers warning of the worst and blaming the other side for problems that have developed. To win public support for their position, they also may advertise, as the hospital workers in New York did.

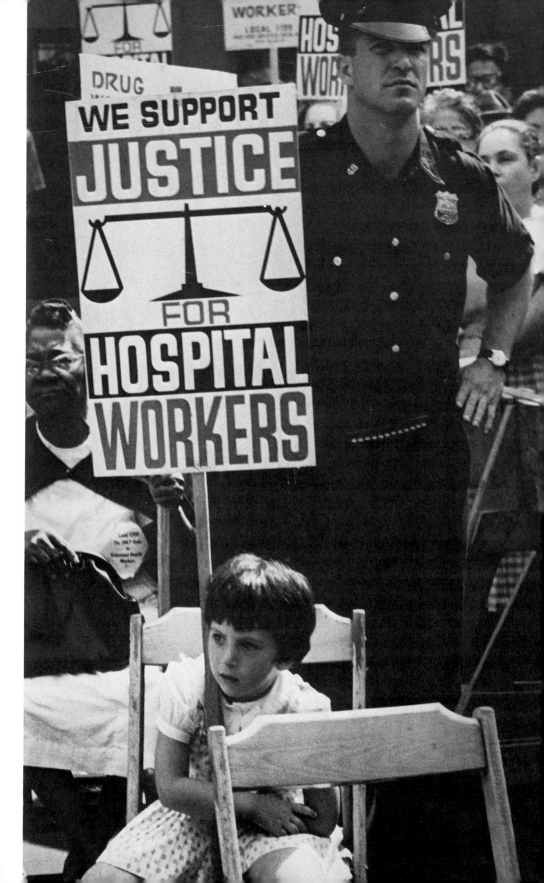

DRUG

WE SUPPORT
JUSTICE
FOR
HOSPITAL
WORKERS

WORKER
LOCAL 1199

HOS
WOR

"We care for the patients, clean the rooms and prepare the food," their ad in the *New York Times* said. "We do the thousand and one things without which these hospitals cannot function. Yet we cannot support our families on the wages we are paid. Most of us are black or Puerto Rican. But all of us are poor. And we've had enough of that. . . ."

If the employer is a government agency, the union may try to pressure the politicians involved through rallies and other publicity techniques. During one negotiation 5000 members of the teachers' union in New York massed outside City Hall and threatened to resign unless pay increases were granted.

"Are you ready to resign?" their president asked.

"Aye," they roared.

"Will you stay out for a week?"

"Yes!"

"For a month?"

"Yes!"

"As long as you have to?"

"Yes!"

But under the goad of an approaching deadline each side becomes more willing to re-examine its position and trade concessions on some issues for gains on others. Day after day, night after night, the two teams discuss, reason, debate, argue. When difficult problems arise, each meets separately, or caucuses, as it is known, to consider the alternatives. When a problem seems insurmountable top officials from both sides meet privately to try to work things out. In most cases, after weeks of effort, the negotiators finally reach agreement, at times only hours before the existing contract expires. The union leaders then submit the results of their efforts to the members. If they approve, a new contract is signed.

A rally in support of a demand for
higher wages by New York hospital workers.

Why Not Split the Difference?

In bargaining over a new contract, a union with 1000 members demands a wage increase of 30 cents an hour or $12 a week. The employer counters with an offer of 10 cents an hour or $4 a week. The difference in their positions represents roughly $400 a year in more income for each worker and $400,000 a year in more expense for the employer. The two sides could agree at the outset to split the difference, compromise on a raise of 20 cents an hour, and thereby save everyone involved a lot of time and trouble. But neither would agree to such an arrangement and for good reason.

Through shrewd bargaining one side or the other might do better. By exploiting its advantages, the union might be able to win 25 cents an hour or $100 a year more than 20 cents would yield. Or because of its strength the company might be able to hold the raise to 15 cents and thereby save $100,000 a year.

If the negotiators decided initially to split the difference, the union's members and the company's stockholders rightly might wonder if they had not been shortchanged. In the end the two sides actually might compromise on a 20-cent raise. But enough is at stake to make the long hours of bargaining worthwhile.

However, some labor relations experts are not impressed with these methods. They say that many issues are too complicated to be handled intelligently with a deadline only hours away, that important decisions at times are made without the information or discussion they require. To avoid such situations and reduce the possibility of strikes, a number of companies and unions now begin bargaining a half year or more before a contract expires. A few also have turned to continuous bargaining. Using this technique, the two sides appoint a committee that studies difficult problems until a fair solution can be found. To deal with the changes growing out of automation, for example, the Kaiser Steel Company and the United Steelworkers of America formed a committee which spent three years developing approaches to deal with the situation.

The vast majority of negotiations, however, are carried out in the shadow of a looming deadline and at times things do not go particularly well. An employer and a union may have such a serious disagreement that negotiations break down, with the result that a strike or a lockout becomes a serious possibility. Or they may reach an agreement, but the union members may reject it and send their leaders back for a better contract. In such cases one party or both may ask a third party to help them settle the dispute. Usually they turn to the government, either to the Federal Mediation and Conciliation Service or to one of the agencies some thirty states have established for this purpose.

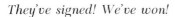

They've signed! We've won!

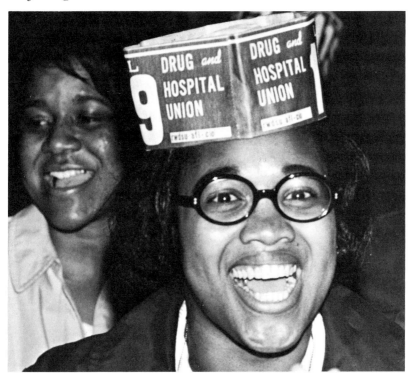

16 | Collective Bargaining: Peace or War?

In a typical year Federal mediators alone try to settle over 8000 disputes that grow out of contract negotiations. They also keep track of thousands of other bargaining sessions to determine whether their help is needed. If trouble erupts and at least one of the parties wants help, a mediator is immediately assigned. In fact, the government may not wait to be invited if the negotiation is vital to the nation's welfare. It may insist on intervening and in the most important situations may rely on the help of officials at the highest levels. In rare cases even cabinet officers and Presidents offer their assistance.

However, there are limits as to what a mediator can do. One thing he cannot do is insist that the two parties settle their dispute. At best, he can help them reach a compromise. In fact, the only power a mediator has is rooted in experience, reason, and patience. In some cases he needs but a few days or weeks to achieve his goal. In others there may be months of daily discussion, and the result still may be failure.

His first task is to understand the dispute. During several meetings he tries to clarify the disagreements that separate the two and determine how important each issue is. One mediator I interviewed helped settle 182 separate issues in a single dispute, but usually far fewer are involved. In the early stages he typically concentrates on the least controversial problems, reasoning that a series of quick agreements will narrow the conflict and encourage further progress. At this point he may do little more than suggest proposals and counterproposals, make sure that everyone speaks in turn, and guard against shouting, name calling, and other disruption.

When he encounters a serious disagreement, usually he changes his tactics. To avoid destructive arguments that could hamper progress, he moves each side's negotiators to a separate room. There, with his guidance and without the need to commit themselves, they review approaches that might solve the problem. Management might decide, for example, that it would be willing to raise its wage offer if the union dropped some of its minor demands. The mediator then reports this to the union's negotiators. If his luck holds, he might be told, "Well, O.K., we really don't care that much if we can get more money." The mediator then passes the word to management.

When the time is ripe, he brings the two sides together again to resume negotiations on a face-to-face basis. In such cases an important issue may be settled immediately. Or it may be dropped when no headway is made, then later reconsidered from a different angle. Depending on his sense of what is needed to achieve agreement, a mediator may play a passive or an active role. If tempers flare once too often, for example, he may halt negotiations for a day or two to give the negotiators a chance to cool down. If a new roadblock arises he may appoint a committee to study the problem. In some cases he may insist that the negotiators continue their bargaining even though the hour is late, on the theory that it is easier to reason with a man who is tired than with one who is not. Or he may take quite a different approach.

"I just start wrapping up my papers and sticking them in my briefcase," one told me. "And somebody'll say, 'What are you doing?' and I'll say, 'Hell, you guys are going to strike anyway so why waste my time?'" And in some cases they ask him to stay, but in others they do not.

FACT-FINDERS AND ARBITRATORS

If the two sides have not settled their argument by the time the old contract expires, the usual result is a strike. But in some cases they extend the deadlines and continue their search for a solution. If they fail and there is a strike, and it seriously affects the public, the government may insist they submit the dispute to a group of fact-finders. These experts try to determine the basic causes of the quarrel, then recommend a solution which either side is free to reject. When a nationwide strike appears likely, the President also may declare an eighty-day "cooling off" period during which the two sides must continue to bargain and the union cannot strike. But if the dispute still cannot be settled, the workers then are free to leave their jobs.

In some cases the final step in the search for peace is arbitration. Each side presents its arguments to a professional arbitrator who weighs the evidence, then reaches a verdict the two agree in advance to accept. If, for example, the dispute involves the size of a wage increase, the arbitrator hears the arguments, then renders a decision which becomes part of the contract. In the end, neither side may get precisely what it wants, but a strike is averted. A number of unions and employers traditionally rely on such an arrangement. Moreover, governments at every level encourage the use of arbitration when a strike threatens a vital service.

In a recent year leading members of management and labor explored ways of increasing the voluntary use of arbitration, but the effort stirred little enthusiasm in their ranks. Many employers and unions already rely on this method to settle grievances on the job, but they are not anxious to give an outsider with little knowledge of their field the final word in decisions that have an important impact on their operations (see chapter 7).

However, arbitration is popular with the public. People see it as an efficient means of settling disputes that otherwise could cause widespread disruption. "When bargaining, mediation, and fact-finding fail, what is the alternative?" they ask. Both labor leaders and managers contend that the economic pressures of a strike eventually produce a settlement acceptable to both sides, that rarely is an arbitrator close enough to a dispute to make a decision that takes into account the long-term needs of both. But the public is not impressed with such arguments, particularly when its transportation, food supply, heat, or garbage collection is threatened. In fact, many people would be pleased to see all strikes banned and all contract disputes submitted to compulsory arbitration. In a nationwide survey one high school student in three favored this approach.

Under compulsory arbitration all major disputes must be

settled by a government arbitrator and all strikes growing out of such disputes are banned. It is a system that has been used for years and with mixed results in Canada, Australia, New Zealand, and a number of European countries. Although it reduces the number of serious strikes, it does not eliminate them. When an arbitrator's "award" does not meet the workers' needs or expectations, often they strike despite the law. At this writing compulsory arbitration is rarely used in the United States. Some states and cities insist that disputes involving public services be submitted to an arbitrator. Congress has passed laws imposing contract settlements when railroads and railroad unions could not agree. But there are few other such examples.

In fact, opposition to compulsory arbitration in this country is heated. Labor relations experts argue it would mean the end of collective bargaining, for the incentive labor and management now have to work out their problems on their own would be removed. They also see government control of wages and prices as another result which, they say, could destroy the free enterprise system. There are those who do not agree with this reasoning, but labor leaders and managers could not agree more.

17 | Strike!

The year this was written sanitation workers in Atlanta went on strike. So did hospital workers in Charleston, blind craftsmen in St. Louis, actors on Broadway, singers at the Metropolitan Opera, reporters for the *Los Angeles Herald-Examiner,* policemen and firemen in Youngstown, Ohio, teachers in Minot, North Dakota, gravediggers in New York, and electrical workers, airline stewardesses, and postmen throughout the country. Two and a half million workers walked off their jobs that year in 5000 strikes. In all, 49 million days of work were lost along with uncounted wages and profits.

From these statistics it might seem that labor was on a rampage or that management had engaged in widespread provocations, but neither was the case. It was a typical year in labor–management relations. Of the tens of thousands of contract negotiations about 5 per cent resulted in strikes. Of the 80 million workers in the labor force, about 4 per cent walked off the job. Of the time available for work that year, about three-tenths of 1 per cent was not used as a result of strikes.

When the size of the United States, its huge labor force, and its complex economy are taken into account, the number of strikes is surprisingly low. In fact, the high school students I questioned estimated there were three to six times as many strikes each year as actually occur. But those that do take place mean hardship for the strikers, economic loss for their employers, and in some cases inconvenience or hardship for the public. A few even threaten the nation's security.

Most of the strikes that year were local affairs. They affected one business or one government agency, involved at most a few hundred workers, and attracted little attention. In fact, two thirds lasted less than two weeks. However, there are strikes that seem as if they will never end. The strike against the General Electric Company described in chapter 1 took almost four months to settle. A nationwide strike against the copper industry closed the mines, smelters, and refineries for almost nine months. One of the longest, most bitter strikes in modern history involved a Wisconsin plumbing manufacturer, the Kohler Company, and its 3000 employees. The strike began in 1954 over the company's refusal to grant a wage increase and a pension. But when Kohler fired the strike leaders, evicted the strikers from their company-owned homes, brought in nonunion workers, and refused to bargain, an ordinary economic strike became a deeply emotional struggle. By the time the strike finally ended, eleven years, eight months, and thirteen days had come and gone.

˙Strikes have their roots in all kinds of situations. A great many grow out of contract negotiations. But others result from efforts to organize a local union or from grievances employees have about working conditions. Some unions also strike out of sympathy with others that have walked off the job.˙Because a union starts a strike, however, does not necessarily mean that it caused the strike. There are times when a strong employer deliberately may provoke a strike to destroy a local union. When the workers leave their jobs, he replaces them with strikebreakers, then bides his time until the union exhausts its resources, and he is rid of it once and for all. In other cases often it is difficult to determine just who is to blame, for management can be as stubborn as labor. However, when one side refuses to compromise any further, a strike may be the only possible result.

WHO WILL WEAKEN?

The decision to strike may be a matter of strategy or a response to pressures over which a union has no control. But usually it comes as no surprise. The conditions and resentments out of which a strike grows are likely to have existed for some time. Moreover, the decision itself usually is made days in advance. If but one local union is involved, the members debate the issue, then vote. If they decide to strike, their international union then must give its permission. If a number of local unions are affected, each may send a representative to a meeting at which the decision is made. In still other cases an international makes the decision on its own. However, there also are times when these procedures are ig-

---

What Would You Do?

Strikes raise hard questions even for those who are not directly involved. For example:

You work in an office where there is a union, but you are not a member. The union goes on strike. Do you cross its picket line to get to your job or do you stay home until the strike ends?

You work on an assembly line in a factory. Your union negotiates a new contract. But another union in the plant fails to do so and strikes. Your leaders urge that you join their members in a sympathy strike. Do you follow their advice or do you continue to work?

The clerks in the supermarket where you regularly shop strike for a higher wage. But the store remains open for business. Do you cross the picket line or do you shop elsewhere?

---

nored. A group of workers may be so enraged by their employer's actions that they walk off their jobs without consulting anyone. But whether a strike is official or a wildcat, it marks the beginning of a war of attrition in which each side tries to grind the other down. In some cases the war turns out to be a skirmish that is settled quickly. But in others it has serious consequences for everyone involved.

As in every war there are preparations to be made. Each side must form a strike organization to deal with strategy, finances, propaganda, and other matters. In every case a union's strategy is to punish the employer so severely that he will grant demands that earlier he rejected. By withholding its labor it tries to cripple his operations. By picketing his facilities it tries to keep nonunion workers from their jobs and customers from his offices or stores. By organizing a boycott, it tries to cut his business still further.

How successful it is depends, of course, on how long an employer can tolerate such pressures. But it also depends on other things. One is money, for without an income no one can strike for very long. To help their members make ends meet, some international unions pay a strike benefit which ranges typically from ten to fifty dollars a week. A local union may try to supplement this by soliciting money and food from other local unions and by getting its members temporary jobs. But when a strike fund runs out or when there is none to begin with, a union is vulnerable.

Time is another factor. A strike may isolate a worker who earlier had led a busy, productive life. Manning a picket line and attending strike meetings may take but a few of his hours each week. Moreover, the bargaining sessions so crucial to his future are secret and the bulletins both sides issue often say nothing. If he does not find another job, and most strikers do not, inevitably the strike becomes a waiting game, a bleak period of empty days marked by growing need. At such times a worker's loyalty to his union may be severely tested.

If an employer closes down his operations a strike is likely to be a quiet affair. Pickets may patrol in front of empty buildings and management may issue statements attacking the union and urging workers to return to their jobs. In such situations it is at the bargaining table that the conflict is joined. If an employer tries to remain in operation, however, a strike may be quite different. As nonunion workers move through picket lines to their jobs there may be name calling, scuffles, even fist fights. Frequently an employer will turn to the police for protection and to a court to limit the number of pickets. If he tries to replace strikers with nonunion

STICKER	DEFECTOR

My feet ache.
My back is wet
With summer sweat.
  My neck hurts.
I curse the fool who tied my sign
With such coarse twine.
  Relief is late.
Yet, Picket Cap' makes light of it.
"Quit, you martyr, quit!"
	Ben returned to work, you say?
	  Not Ben! Not him!
	A scab's another kind of being:
	The yellow streak, receding chin—
	  Not Ben. Can't be Ben.
	A friend, a rock, a leader gone
	Without a word to anyone.
	At once your world is turned to dust.
	What can you believe?
	Whom can you trust?

MARSHALL DUBIN
Local 1199, Drug and Hospital Union

workers—"scabs," as unionists call them—frayed tempers may touch off an even more serious conflict.

What happened at Iowa Beef Processors in Dakota City, Nebraska, is an example. When 1100 workers struck for higher wages, the company flew in hundreds of Mexican–Americans to take their place. To keep union pickets at bay, it also brought in state troopers, armed guards, and police dogs, and distributed tear gas pens to its managers. But as the weeks dragged by and frustrations grew, trouble came to those on both sides of the strike. Automobile tires were slashed, power lines into the plant were cut, houses were dynamited, and men were beaten and shot.

If its members give in, a strike may severely weaken a union, even destroy it. A two-month strike all but destroyed a teachers' union in East St. Louis, Illinois, when a lack of income forced its members to return to work and the school board stripped them of tenure and other privileges they had fought hard to win. Or the losses a company suffers may drive it out of business. After a five-month strike, the American Machine and Foundry Company had no choice but to close a bowling-equipment plant in Brooklyn, New York, which cost six hundred strikers their jobs. But far more often economic pressures eventually produce a reasonable settlement, and the two sides return to work. But seldom are things ever the same.

"I WILL HOLD SCHOOL UNTIL 10:30 TOMORROW AND THEN SEND THE CHILDREN HOME"

When a man named Tadgh Hanna walked off his job a few years ago, it was the first time a teacher went on strike in the state of Maine. Hanna taught in the one-room school on the island of Matinicus twenty-two miles from the mainland. He had asked repeatedly that the citizens repair the schoolhouse, improve the outhouses, build a playground, buy new supplies, and hire a school nurse and a janitor, but each time they ignored his requests. When he presented his plan again at the school's annual budget meeting and once more it was rejected, he decided to strike. He informed the town of his decision two days later through an announcement in the local newspaper. "I will hold school until 10:30 tomorrow morning and then send the children home," he declared. "The school shall remain closed until the Maine Department of Education corrects the deplorable conditions."

When 160,000 poorly paid postmen went on strike for wage increases in that period, it was the first time a large group struck against the Federal government. But the postmen felt they had no choice. "We are not militants," one explained. "We're just human beings that want to live normally. I've got six children and the only way we can live is for me to work overtime and for my wife to take a job in a button factory."

When 10,000 sanitation workers in New York walked off their jobs, however, they had no reasonable explanation. Their leaders had agreed to the same wage increase other city employees had accepted. But the union's members wanted even more, and they struck for it with almost disastrous results. During the nine days they remained away from work, 100,000 tons of garbage collected on the sidewalks of the city. As the piles grew, so did the threat from disease and fire. When the mayor spoke of bringing in the state's National Guard to remove the garbage, the Central Labor Council in the city threatened that hundreds of thousands of other unionists would strike if he did so, and bring the gov-

ernment to its knees. In the end the union got what it wanted.

In many respects strikes against the government closely resemble those against private employers. However, workers in the private sector have the right to strike. As noted earlier, those in the public sector generally do not. When a government worker walks off the job, therefore, he usually breaks the law.

When the Boston police struck for higher wages in 1919, Calvin Coolidge, then governor of Massachusetts, promptly fired them and brought in the National Guard. "There is no right to strike against the public safety by anybody anywhere any time," he declared. Most lawmakers today agree. They maintain that a government must protect itself against groups with the power to jeopardize the public welfare, or chaos will result. Thus, firemen, policemen, sanitation workers, welfare workers, teachers, and others who strike may be fined, fired, or jailed, or all three. In addition, their unions may be fined thousands of dollars a day and their leaders may be imprisoned.

Although every government vigorously opposes strikes, through their laws some encourage them. On the theory that they cannot share their power with any group, a number of states refuse to bargain with their employees and do not permit local governments to bargain with theirs. In a few cases they even deny them the right to organize unions. In such situations public employees usually have little or no voice in decisions that affect their jobs. In fact, when they have serious grievances often their only alternative is to break the law and strike.

There are a growing number of states, however, that have given public employees the right to bargain collectively. Usually such states also have a procedure for settling dis-

The result of a strike by New York's 10,000 garbage collectors.

putes relying first on mediation, then on fact-finding, and in a few cases, as a last resort, on arbitration. But even in such situations government unions insist they need the right to strike, for without this "club in the closet" negotiations are no more than conversations in which a government can, if it wishes, make all the decisions.

Union leaders acknowledge that there are vital services, such as police and fire protection, where strikes cannot be tolerated. In fact, the American Federation of State, County and Municipal Workers expels policemen, firemen, and prison guards who strike. But when negotiations with teachers, transit workers, welfare workers, and others are involved, the unions insist they need the same rights as workers in the private sector. In some situations experience bears them out, for only through striking have they been able to obtain justice. But there are cases in which unions of public employees have used the strike irresponsibly to gain whatever they can no matter what the consequences, much as New York's sanitation workers did.

Each year a great many negotiations in the public sector are settled peacefully. But each year there also are hundreds of illegal strikes which grow out of contract disputes or efforts to organize unions where they are banned. Although there are penalties, those who strike clearly feel that the price is not too great to pay. When 160,000 postal workers struck, they faced loss of their jobs, a $1000 fine, and a year in jail, all of which the government agreed to overlook when the dispute finally was settled. But Tadgh Hanna lost his job for striking against the citizens of Matinicus, and 1400 sanitation workers lost theirs for striking against the city of Atlanta. When the garbage collectors in New York struck, their president was jailed for fifteen days. When the teachers' union in Newark, New Jersey, went on strike, 206 unionists were arrested, including several who were grandmothers. When the president of the American Federation of Teachers journeyed to Newark to walk with them on the picket line, he also was arrested and spent forty-eight days behind bars.

Labor relations experts do not see a quick end to such situations. Although progress is being made, they say that in some areas it may be years before changes in attitudes and laws make it possible for governments and their employees to work out their differences peacefully and fairly.

18 | Politics

Soon after Richard Nixon took office as President of the United States, he invited labor's top officials to the White House to discuss their goals. Later he courted them at luncheons and dinners and even arranged a military pageant in their honor on Labor Day. Although he did not share many of their objectives, he understood well their political influence.

Political action is as important to labor as is collective bargaining, for it is in the Congress and the state legislatures that the unions attempt to win what they cannot gain in contract negotiations. The changes they seek range from social improvements and greater protection against economic insecurity to expanded rights in organizing and bargaining. Whether they succeed or fail depends, of course, on the lawmakers. As a result, they also work hard to elect men and women who support their goals. But these tactics are not labor's alone. Businessmen, farmers, conservationists, veterans, and other pressure groups also use them to meet their objectives. What is unusual about labor's political program is its size, which is second only to that of the business community, and its considerable success.

Labor's concern with politics dates to the early days of unionism. In the 1820s a group in Philadelphia organized the Workingmen's Party, the world's first political party whose goal it was to improve the lot of workers (see chapter 3). Over the years Greenback–Laborites, Socialists, Communists, and coalitions of unionists, liberals, and farmers all have formed labor parties. But unlike similar groups in Europe, none succeeded in attracting large numbers of union members (see chapter 19). Nor is it likely that a labor party would succeed today in the United States, for most American workers do not regard themselves as permanent members of a working class. As they see it, their interests are better served by a large, broadly based party, such as the Democrats or the Republicans, than by one concerned with the interests of but a single group.

The political strategy unions follow today actually was decided in 1908 when Samuel Gompers urged that unions "stand faithfully" by their "friends" and "oppose and defeat" their "enemies." But it was not until the 1930s when union membership and union treasuries swelled to undreamed of size that the labor movement became a force no politician could ignore.

DEMOCRATS AND REPUBLICANS

The executive board of the AFL–CIO decides which candidates the giant federation will back for President and Vice-President. The state labor federations decide whom labor will support for Congress and various state offices, a decision that usually is made at a statewide convention of delegates from local unions. Inevitably most of labor's endorsements go to liberal politicians who, with their interest in social reform, traditionally have been labor's "friends." Since most liberals are Democrats it is the Democratic Party that usually receives labor's support.

If anyone doubts the wisdom of this strategy, he need only review the periodic reports the AFL–CIO issues on how Congressmen vote. A recent report listed 119 Congressmen who had voted "right" on each of thirteen bills of importance to labor. Of the 119, 116 were Democrats. Individual unions, the internationals and the locals, also endorse candidates for office, but most follow the lead of the federations. The major exceptions usually are the construction unions, which are among the most conservative labor organizations and traditionally back Republicans.

Labor's political operations are handled by the AFL–CIO's Committee on Political Education, or COPE as it is better known. From its headquarters in Washington, D.C., it directs a nationwide network of campaign committees. During a major election they operate in every state, every major city, and most Congressional districts. Together they comprise one of the largest and most effective political organizations in the country. International unions outside the AFL–CIO have political organizations of their own, whose operations are modeled after those of COPE.

When a candidate receives labor's endorsement he can count on a financial contribution to help cover his expenses.

CONGRESSIONAL DISTRICT	PELLY (R)	MEEDS (D)	HANSEN (D)	MAY (R)	FOLEY (D)	HICKS (D)	ADAMS (D)
	1	2	3	4	5	6	7
1. 14(b) Repeal (Procedural Vote)	W	R	R	W	R	R	R
2. 14(b) Repeal (Effort to Kill)	R	R	R	W	R	R	R
3. 14(b) Repeal (Passage)	R	R	R	W	R	R	R
4. Minimum Wage	R	R	R	W	R	R	R
5. House Rules	W	R	R	W	R	R	R
6. Aid to Education	W	R	R	W	R	R	R
7. Medicare	W	R	R	W	R	R	R
8. Housing Department, City Aid	W	R	R	W	R	R	R
9. Housing, Rent Subsidies	W	R	R	W	W	W	R
10. Voting Rights	W	R	R	–	R	R	R
11. War on Poverty	W	R	R	W	R	R	R
12. Public Works	–	R	R	W	R	W	R
13. Public Power	W	R	R	W	R	R	R
RIGHT	22	13	34	4	12	11	13
WRONG	46	0	0	40	1	2	0

How members of the House of Representatives from Washington state voted on thirteen bills the AFL–CIO regarded as crucial to labor's welfare. Votes marked "W" were "wrong" votes, according to the Federation. Those marked "R" were "right." The totals at the bottom also include votes on labor issues in previous years.

He also may receive help with his campaign from union volunteers. In addition, many union members may vote for him, but this is something he cannot count on, for unionists are as independent as other voters. In the end, their needs, hopes, and fears determine how they vote. Frequently a union endorsement reflects these. But when it does not, their votes may go to another candidate. Many blue collar workers, for example, reject the liberal candidates labor proposes. Threatened by the rising aspirations of the black community, they give their support instead to politicians who promise to keep the black man "in his place." But even in such situations a union endorsement is nothing to be scorned.

MONEY AND MANPOWER

When President Franklin D. Roosevelt ran for re-election in 1936 the unions contributed $770,000 to help him campaign. It was labor's first major financial contribution to a political candidate and led to a widespread demand by business that future contributions be banned. The result was a Federal law which placed the same restrictions on unions that for years had applied to corporations. Today neither can use funds from their treasuries to back candidates for Federal office. Instead each year COPE conducts a drive among union members to raise money it needs for its operations. Although most members contribute but a few dollars, their total contribution is substantial. In a recent year they gave $7 million to help candidates for President, Vice-President, and Congress, or a third of all the money spent in those races.

It is likely that labor spent as much that year on state and local elections. But in such races Federal restrictions do not apply, with the result that the money needed came directly from union treasuries. Some union members object to having their dues spent to support men and women they oppose, but usually there is little they can do about it.

How much labor spends in a particular race varies with the candidate and his chances of winning. During one election campaign in Wisconsin labor organizations gave over $200,000 to eighteen candidates. These contributions ranged from $500 to a weak candidate for the House of Representatives to $51,000 for Democratic Senator William Proxmire, who was seeking re-election. In a major contest labor money may come from all over the country. In Senator Proxmire's case, the Steelworkers, Pipefitters, Seafarers, Electrical Workers, Auto Workers, Textile Workers, Furniture Workers, and Railway Clerks all made contributions. Their reasons were as practical as could be.

In an important race labor also may help in other ways. It may prepare campaign literature for a candidate, place newspaper advertisements in his behalf, provide sound trucks, and arrange for radio and television commercials. It also may organize rallies and parades. It even may help run a campaign. When Ross Bass sought the Democratic nomination for United States Senator from Tennessee, local labor leaders served as his campaign managers, and experts were dispatched from COPE headquarters in Washington to help win the black vote. One of the most valuable contributions labor makes is getting out the vote. In important races union volunteers canvass door to door in advance of an election to encourage people who have not registered to do so and thereby qualify to vote. Then on election day they remind them to cast their ballots and if necessary serve as baby-sitters or drive them to the polls. When Hubert Humphrey ran for President in 1968, 190,000 union members across the country helped in this way.

In many elections it is hard to gauge just how much of an impact labor has. But there are situations when its influence is clear. John F. Kennedy's election as President was due in large part to an extraordinary registration drive in which labor and the Democratic party worked as partners. Together they registered millions of new voters. In Philadelphia alone 160,000 new Democrats were added to the voting rolls as a result of their efforts. In the twenty-two states where Kennedy's margin of victory was under 2 per cent, experts say it was the newly registered voters who made the difference.

Labor also has had a significant impact on our political

TOP: *Union volunteers telephone union members on Election Day to encourage them to vote.* BOTTOM: *Members of the International Ladies' Garment Workers' Union march in support of the Democratic candidate for governor in New York State.*

system. In traditionally conservative midwestern states like Ohio, Indiana, and Michigan, its efforts in behalf of liberal candidates have created a two-party system. Prior to the rise of unionism in such areas, voters who were not Republicans had no voice in their government and the Democratic party was not strong enough to give them one.

THE LABOR LOBBY

In the nation's capital there are about one hundred men and women whose job it is to work for laws that benefit the labor movement and fight those that threaten labor's interests. In the state capitals hundreds of others have the same assignment. All work behind the scenes, encouraging lawmakers to support or oppose various bills. In some cases they even prepare the legislation labor needs, then see to it that it is introduced. Many of these lobbyists represent major international unions. The rest are on the staff of the AFL–CIO or the state labor federations. However, their tactics are not different from those of the hundreds of lobbyists for business organizations who oppose them.

Union lobbyists closely follow the progress of every bill that could affect the labor movement.* When such legislation is "in committee" they may call on the committee members to state their case. If hearings are scheduled, they may arrange for labor leaders to testify and even prepare their testimony. If the bill reaches the legislature, the lobbyists may visit scores of lawmakers to plead their cause. In some cases they present their arguments and leave. But if they

---

* Typically a bill is first considered by a legislative committee. If a major law is involved, the committee holds hearings at which interested groups may testify. If the committee approves the bill, it then goes to the full legislature for consideration.

need support badly enough they may resort to other tactics.

They may try to strike a bargain. If a lawmaker agrees to support their measure, they may agree to support one of his. In other cases they may exert pressure of various kinds. They may recall favors labor has done for him. They may arrange for labor leaders to telephone him or visit him. They may see to it that union members from his area write him letters asking that he back the bill involved. Or they may promise increased support when he seeks re-election if he helps them or threaten him with opposition if he does not.

When an issue of widespread concern develops, labor's lobbyists may join forces with lobbyists from other groups. This happened when President Nixon asked the Senate to approve his nomination of Federal Judge Clement F. Haynsworth, Jr., for the United States Supreme Court. The AFL–CIO regarded Haynsworth as antilabor. Civil rights organizations regarded him as antiblack. Together these groups fought the nomination, which in the end was rejected.

Inevitably labor's lobbying grows out of labor's problems. When clothing made with cheap foreign labor began to flood American stores, many garment workers in this country lost their jobs and labor campaigned to ban such imports. When owners of American merchant ships registered their vessels in other countries to avoid high union wages, labor sought laws to prevent them from doing so. However, much of the legislation it seeks deals with social problems that affect all of us. So great is its emphasis on improving health care, housing, and education, that liberals regard it as one of the most progressive forces for change in the country.

Yet many of the same people are dismayed by the foreign policies for which labor also has lobbied, particularly its rigid anti-Communism, which excludes any cooperation with

*AFL–CIO lobbyists urge a committee of the House
of Representatives to support a higher minimum wage.*

Communist nations. Nowhere, not even in the most conservative organizations, is one likely to find a more dedicated group of anti-Communists than labor's top leaders. As one explained, ". . . Where workers lose their freedom, where they do under the control of a dictatorship . . . this represents a threat to all of us. When Communist governments increase in number . . . the threat grows."

The AFL–CIO's Department of International Relations, headed when this was written by a militant anti-Communist who once headed the American Communist Party, helps determine labor's foreign policies, then pressures the government to adopt them. And often the government listens. Labor takes positions on nations the United States should befriend, those it should assist, and those with whom it should trade. It also speaks out on matters of peace and war. Thus, the AFL–CIO was one of the most persistent supporters of the long, costly war the United States waged against the Communists in Vietnam. Even when much of the nation turned against the war and leaders of many international unions joined them, those at the federation stood fast in the belief that Communism had to be defeated at any cost (see chapter 19).

For the most part, however, labor's programs originate in resolutions union members debate and approve at union conventions. Translating a resolution into law is not easy, but labor has had some impressive achievements. It is doubtful, for example, that health insurance for the aged, protection for consumers against fraud, Federal aid to education, and other legislation we take for granted would have been enacted so promptly without its leadership. This also is true of laws that protect the rights of blacks and other racial minorities in voting, finding jobs, and obtaining decent housing. At one point a group of Southern Congressmen offered labor a deal regarding civil rights legislation. If it would reduce its pressure for more liberal laws, they would oppose a bill that would sharply restrict union activities. But labor refused to cooperate and the Landrum–Griffin Bill was enacted (see chapter 11). In the years that followed, however, so were the major civil rights acts that spurred a black revolution.

The labor lobby's agenda in Washington was crowded at this writing. It included increased Social Security payments for the aged, a national health-insurance program, improved transportation facilities in metropolitan areas, day-care centers for children with working mothers, and laws that would give farm workers the same right to organize unions and bargain that other workers won in 1935. By the time you read this, some of these efforts may have borne fruit.

19 | Unions Abroad

Over 200 million workers throughout the world are union members. But their unions are strikingly different, varying with their government, its economy, and the tradition of freedom in their country. In industrialized nations like England and Sweden they are well-established organizations of great importance. In totalitarian countries like Russia and Spain, they have little freedom and little influence. In emerging countries like Kenya and South Vietnam, they are in their infancy, groping, much as their governments, for the power with which to function. (A union meeting in South Vietnam is shown in the photograph above.)

In most countries, however, workers tend to be more unified than those in the United States. To a greater extent they regard themselves as members of a single working class with common interests and goals. As a result, many nations have a far higher proportion of union members. In the United States less than 30 per cent of the work force belongs to unions. But in England it is 40 per cent; in Italy, 50 per cent; in Australia, 60 per cent; in Israel and Sweden, over 70 per cent.

Unions abroad also rely far more on politics to achieve their goals than is the case here. One reason is that their governments often assume greater responsibility for social and economic problems. But another is that collective bargaining frequently does not work as well as it does in the United States. Usually there are no laws which require that an employer bargain with a union. Even when negotiations do take place, there may be no way to win concessions if an employer is not willing to grant them, for most foreign unions do not have the money to strike for very long. In Japan, for example, strikes by teachers' unions traditionally last but an hour or two, serving more as a symbol of discontent than as a means of economic pressure. Using another tactic, some French workers lock their employers in their offices until they are willing to compromise on their demands or until the police intervene. But more often unions abroad turn to their governments for the gains they seek.

Almost every country has a labor federation which speaks for its unions on matters of national importance, much as the AFL–CIO does in the United States. In England it is the Trades Union Congress. In Japan it is the Japanese Confederation of Labor. In Israel it is Histradrut. In Canada there are two such groups, the larger of which by far is the Canadian Labor Congress, which has close ties to the AFL–CIO.

Along with their other duties, labor federations abroad frequently function as political parties or form close alliances with existing parties. The Labour party in England, for example, is the result of a merger between the Socialist party and the Trades Union Congress. However, at times a federation turns to the right rather than to the left to win the goals it seeks. In Argentina, for example, the unions kept the Nazi-style dictator Juan Perón in power for almost a decade. Although Peron destroyed liberty in his country, he saw to it that unionists got regular wage increases, for which they were willing to trade their freedom.

Many countries have two or more labor federations that compete for members and for influence. Usually they are allied with rival political parties. Frequently one is tied to the Communists and at least one other to an anti-Communist group. Such organizations compete in Italy, France, and many of the emerging nations of Latin America, Africa, and Asia. In fact, their struggle for power often is an element in the cold war between Communist nations and those of the free world, for a labor movement with political muscle can influence which side an uncommitted country will befriend. (See the later section "The United States Government, the AFL–CIO, and Communism.")

Along with improved wages, union members in many countries seek changes in the economic and political systems that govern their lives. When the Labour party first won control of the government in England, it nationalized basic industries and established free health insurance in line with its traditional goals. When the Communists and the unions that gave them their major support came to power in Chile, there were similar changes. After the Second World War, the unions in many European colonies spearheaded campaigns which won independence for their nations. In the process a number of labor leaders became national leaders. In the Caribbean, Alexander Bustamente of Jamaica rose to power this way. In Africa, so did Tom Mboya of Kenya and Sékou Touré of Guinea. By contrast, unions in the United States are not concerned with changing the nation's political or economic structure. "We like the system the way it is," an official of the AFL–CIO said. "We just want it to pay off better."

If unions abroad do not have the political power to win the changes they seek, and these are of great importance, they may turn as a last resort to a general strike in which members of all unions stop work, a tactic virtually unknown in the United States. (In 1919 Seattle was crippled by a general strike. In 1934 so was San Francisco. But these were rare events.) If successful, such a strike can paralyze a city or an entire nation. In a recent year, for example, unions in Italy organized a general strike to force their government to

deal with a severe housing shortage. During the day and night it lasted, 10 million workers, half the Italian labor force, walked off their jobs. All work came to a halt in Rome, Naples, Milan, and other cities and, with chaos as the alternative, the government agreed to act. In France that year a general strike over economic conditions caused the government's leaders to resign and forced the election of a new president.

There is one other crucial difference between unions abroad and those in the United States. It involves the freedom to join a union, to bargain with an employer, and to strike. In this country, the law guarantees these rights to most workers. In other nations where such rights exist, they do so by virtue of tradition, but usually they are not protected by law. In nations where a dictator seizes power, the rights to form a union and to strike are typically among the first to be curtailed. In fact, the unions themselves may be dissolved, for, as we have seen, a major strike can bring a government to its knees.

Unions in most Communist countries do not pose such a threat, however, for they serve as agencies of the government. In Russia one of their tasks is to protect workers against unjust decisions by managers. But their most important job is to keep production at a high level. When the government decided to crack down on workers who were shirking their responsibilities, it was the local unions that ferreted them out and punished them. Some lost bonuses, vacations, and seniority they had accumulated over long years. The worst offenders were expelled from their unions and, as a result, lost all their benefits.

Italian workers block rail traffic during a
general strike in which ten million men and women
walked off their jobs to protest government policies.

WFTU, ICFTU, CISC

Depending on its political position, a labor federation also may ally itself with a global labor organization. Communist federations join the World Federation of Trade Unions (WFTU), which represents labor organizations in 40 countries throughout the Communist world. On the other hand, anti-Communist federations usually join the International Confederation of Free Trade Unions (ICFTU), which represents 120 labor organizations. The two work to build labor movements that reflect their political ideas, with the result that they are fierce rivals in the cold war. A third global organization also competes vigorously for members, but it is not directly involved in this conflict. It is a Catholic group, the International Confederation of Christian Trade Unions (in French, CISC).

The three organizations barely are known in the United States or other industrialized areas, but they have an important impact in newly developing nations. They train union leaders in their brand of unionism, give funds and technical help to unions they support, operate trade schools for their members, and in some cases become deeply involved in the power struggles within a government. They also operate worldwide "secretariats" that concentrate on the problems of workers in particular occupations. There are, for example, international secretariats of transport workers, metal workers, miners, teachers, and journalists. As a growing number of employers have developed operations on an international scale, these secretariats have taken on increasing importance.

One of their major jobs is to help unions in emerging countries with contract negotiations. They provide information on contracts negotiated elsewhere, conduct meetings at which workers a company employs in different countries exchange information, and arrange for established unions, including American unions, to help those that lack experience. When workers at the Ford Motor Company's plant in Venezuela bargained over a new contract, for example, an expert from the United Auto Workers journeyed from Detroit to serve as their adviser. A secretariat also may help with strikes against an international employer. If workers in one country walk off the job, it may organize sympathy strikes at the employer's installations in other countries. When American unions strike against an international airline, for example, airport workers in Rome traditionally have refused to permit the company's planes to land. Such actions are unusual, but labor officials foresee a day when they may not be.

THE UNITED STATES GOVERNMENT, THE AFL–CIO, AND COMMUNISM

Caught up as it is in a cold war with Russia, the United States government has a deep interest in unions abroad. For years it has worked to encourage the growth of anti-Communist unions in the emerging countries. Of course, the Russian government has worked just as hard to win unions to its side. In this competition, the American government has depended in part on the ICFTU. But to strengthen its effort, it has relied far more heavily on organizations the AFL–CIO operates, primarily with Federal funds, in Latin America, Africa, and Asia.

The oldest and largest of these is the American Institute for Free Labor Development (AIFLD), which was organized in 1962 in Central and South America after the Communist Fidel Castro seized power in Cuba. The others are the

African–American Labor Center and the Asian–American Free Labor Institute.

AIFLD has operations in nineteen countries with a staff that includes many former union officials from the United States. Each year it spends several million dollars to help anti-Communist unions recruit more members and strengthen their influence with their governments. At education centers it operates throughout Latin America it has taught over 60,-000 workers how to organize and operate labor unions in the American style. A thousand of these workers also have taken advanced training at a school it operates near Washington, D.C.

AIFLD also works to make life better for members of anti-Communist unions with the result that it makes membership in these organizations more appealing. Its major effort involves construction of low-cost housing, of which there is a severe shortage in Latin America. International unions and insurance companies in the United States lend the money needed, and the American government guarantees that it will be repaid. Then AIFLD and the unions involved see to it that the housing is built. In this way over 13,000 members of anti-Communist unions have acquired decent homes for their families.

AIFLD also provides job training for members of unions it favors. It organizes special banks which grant them loans they otherwise could not obtain. It also makes possible hundreds of small improvements that make life more tolerable for workers "on its side." With its help, for example, members of an anti-Communist laborers' union acquired a brick-making machine with which they made the 7000 bricks they needed to build a school for their children.

But there is another, uglier face to this struggle, for the government's Central Intelligence Agency also fights the

*A Bolivian trained by the American Institute
for Free Labor Development urges impoverished
farm workers in his country to organize a union.*

cold war on the labor front. Since it deals with espionage its
operations generally are secret. However, it is known that
they have involved the training of anti-Communist union
leaders and the use of unions in the United States to help
overthrow Communist regimes. The agency played a major
role, for example, in bringing down a Communist regime
in British Guiana (now the independent nation Guyana)
which President John F. Kennedy saw as a serious threat to
American security.

CIA agents first arranged to use an international union in
the United States, the American Federation of State, County
and Municipal Workers (AFSCME), as a base of operations.*

———

* *New York Times,* February 18–22, 1967.

Posing as AFSCME officials, they convinced leaders of government unions in Guiana to strike for better conditions and
to use sabotage, riots, and other violence as weapons. The
agents then furnished money to cover the expenses involved,
advised the leaders on strategy, and even provided medical
supplies for workers who were injured while rioting. The
strike brought down the government, and the threat John
Kennedy saw was eliminated.

Part Five | A LOOK AHEAD

Of the 120 high school students I questioned in writing this book, 48 said they would join a union if they had a choice. Of course, under union security agreements others will join whether or not they want to. In addition, a number will deal with unions from the other side of the bargaining table, as managers, not as members. But what will these unions be like? How will they differ from those we know today? As we have seen, major changes already are taking place.

For one, the labor movement is becoming more representative of the many kinds of workers in this country, with more professional, technical, and white collar workers and a growing number in the service trades. As unions expand into new fields, moreover, they are increasing in size. In a recent four-year period unions in the United States grew by 2 million members. But as they have grown they also have become more bureaucratic, with the result that the individual member has less and less influence in their activities.

When one has learned this much, however, he has approached the limits of what can be assumed about unions in the future. If he seeks more information, he finds questions instead of answers. For example:

Will the labor movement begin in earnest to unionize the poorest of the poor—such as the great mass of farm workers across the country—who are among the most difficult to organize, who yield the smallest return in dues, yet need unions more than anyone else?

Will unions that control the labor supply in a particular craft continue to exercise monopoly power in setting wages and affecting prices?

Will managers in areas such as the South and the Southwest continue to flaunt the legal rights of workers who wish to form unions and bargain collectively? Will the nation's laws be strengthened to prevent such behavior?

Will more government employees, particularly on the state and local levels, win the right to bargain collectively?

Will the nature of collective bargaining change? Will crisis bargaining disappear? Will it be replaced by the continuous bargaining described in chapter 16 or some other method? Will bargaining at the local level decline as larger and larger unions match their strength against larger and larger employers? Will the public gain a direct voice in major decisions, at the bargaining table, since often it is seriously affected by the actions taken?

As society grows more complex and more susceptible to disruption, will the right to strike be further restricted? Will compulsory arbitration, so vigorously opposed by labor and management, finally be used to settle disputes?

Will unions continue indefinitely to win higher wages, better benefits, and a larger voice in the job? Most labor leaders tend to think so, but some scholars are not so sure.

There is one other question that is raised again and again about the future. Will unions retain their strength? At this writing it does not seem possible that unions will lose their influence. If anything, it appears that they may grow stronger. As life has grown more complex and the power of the individual has diminished, group action has become an increasingly effective technique for achieving change, not only in labor–management relations, but in an individual's relations with all institutions. Hemingway put the case well in his novel *To Have and Have Not.* "A man alone doesn't have a chance," he wrote.

CAREERS IN LABOR RELATIONS

TERMS USED IN LABOR RELATIONS

BIBLIOGRAPHY AND SUGGESTED READINGS

INDEX

CAREERS IN LABOR RELATIONS

A number of persons who work in labor relations do so, at least in part, out of a sense of commitment. An official of a major teachers' union told me he saw his job as "helping people to grow, to be more assertive, to be less like lackies, to speak out when they were victims of injustice." A labor relations manager I interviewed saw his job as "preserving harmony," but also as protecting management's "right to manage" against "further incursions" by unions. Of course, in choosing a career one's interests, values, and personality all play a role, and so do money and chance.

Most of the jobs in labor relations are with international unions, labor federations, companies, and government agencies. The men and women involved vary from administrators and organizers to educators, economists, and lawyers, with the result that the educational requirements in this field vary widely. In unions the key qualifications for many jobs are experience as a unionist and an aptitude for leadership. In a number of positions a college degree is useful and in some it is essential. In business and government, on the other hand, most labor relations jobs require training at the college level.

The pay in this field also varies widely, depending not only on the job but on where one works. Salaries in unions tend to be lower than those in government, which in turn are likely to be lower than those in private employment. In a recent year beginning salaries ranged from $7000 in international unions to $10,000 in industry.

For information on career opportunities in unions write the Education Department at the AFL–CIO in Washington or the education director of one or more of the large international unions. Addresses and officials are listed in the annual *Directory of National and International Unions in the United States,* which is available in many libraries. To get a sense of what working for a union might be like, also try to arrange an interview with an official of the central labor council in your area or with an officer of one of the large local unions.

For information on labor relations in business and industry, try to talk with the labor relations or personnel manager at one or more of the large companies where you live. For a picture of opportunities in government, write the public information officer of your state labor department, which usually is in the state capital. Also contact the following Federal agencies:

The Bureau of Labor Statistics, 441 G Street NW, Washington, D.C. 20001; the Federal Mediation and Conciliation Service, Department of Labor Building, Washington, D.C. 20427; the Labor–Management Services Administration, Department of Labor, Washington, D.C. 20210; the National Labor Relations Board, 1717 Pennsylvania Avenue, Washington, D.C.

Jobs with Unions

Business Agents. These are full-time, salaried administrators who supervise the day-to-day activities of one or more local unions. Usually they are union members who are elected to their jobs by their fellow members, then stand for re-election every two or three years. In some local unions the president and the treasurer are also full-time jobs.

Education Specialists. Members of union education departments have two jobs to perform. One is planning and conducting education programs for members of their international union. These range from job training and instruction in how to run a local union to seminars on social issues and the techniques of preparing for retirement. Their other job is the preparation of booklets and films to explain unionism and its goals to the membership. Two thirds of the nation's international unions have education departments. So do the AFL–CIO, most of the state labor federations, a number of central labor councils, and a few of the largest local unions. Training in labor relations and education is ideal preparation for such work.

International Representatives, Organizers. An international representative helps local unions handle contract negotiations, grievances, and other problems. In some international unions he also works as an organizer, helping unorganized workers form new local unions. A number of internationals have full-time organizers but, as suggested in chapter 13, often these are difficult jobs which require unusual dedication to the union cause. At times college graduates start out in such positions. In fact, in some internationals these are the only jobs available to them. But usually a union organizer is a former part-time official of a local union who has decided to make unionism a career. In fact, many of the most important administrative positions in unions are filled by men and women who once were organizers or international representatives.

Lawyers. Ordinarily an international union's attorneys are among the most influential members of its staff. They help union leaders develop policies, sit with them at the bargaining table, represent their union in court and before the National Labor Relations Board, draft laws the union seeks, and in some cases also serve as lobbyists. With the exception of bargaining, the attorneys who work for the labor federations have similar duties.

Public Relations Specialists. Like most organizations, labor unions and labor federations rely on propagandists to win support for their policies and goals. Those employed by an international union ordinarily prepare a newspaper or a monthly magazine for members, prepare speeches for top officials, and deal with newsmen. Some organize the conventions their unions hold periodically. A number carry out the political programs described in chapter 18. Most are journalists with college degrees who once worked for daily newspapers.

Researchers. International unions also rely heavily on economists and statisticians. Their primary job is to provide facts and figures to justify labor's demands at the bargaining table. In some cases they also help determine what the demands will be, particularly when they relate to wage increases, insurance coverage, and pensions. In the labor federations often they are part of the team that drafts new laws labor seeks and helps prepare the testimony labor leaders present before legislative committees.

Jobs with Employers

Labor Relations Specialists. The assignment may be at a corporate headquarters in a large city, at a company's plant in a small town like Loudon, Tennessee, or in the office of a government agency. In each case the job is to represent management's interests in its relationships with its employees. A labor relations specialist will deal with attempts to organize a local union, speak for management when grievances arise on the job, and sit across from labor in negotiating contracts. Usually he holds one or more degrees in labor relations, economics, and/or personnel practices.

Jobs with Government

In this section the jobs described are primarily with the federal agencies responsible for regulating labor–management relations. But the men and women who staff state labor departments often have similar responsibilities. Virtually all such jobs require college degrees and in some cases experience in unions or management as well.

Administrators. These specialists administer the labor laws. They also monitor the state of labor–management relations to determine the need for possible changes in the government's role. Some administrators also serve as negotiators, representing the government in bargaining with its employees.

Economists, Statisticians. One of their primary jobs is recording data on employment, productivity, wages, and other issues in labor–management relations. However, they also analyze the meaning of these statistics, to the extent possible, and anticipate future trends. In the Federal government this work is carried out by the Bureau of Labor Statistics which issues a continuing flood of reports on the state of the economy. (Its regional offices in major cities are excellent resources for students with a serious need for information on the economy.)

Investigators. Those employed by governmental agencies determine if existing laws are being violated. Those who work for the Congressional committees that oversee labor relations help determine if there is a need to change these laws. The committees primarily involved are the Labor and Public Welfare Committee in the Senate and the Education and Labor Committee in the House of Representatives.

Lawyers. Some represent the government in prosecuting alleged violations of labor laws. Others, employed by the National Labor Relations Board, conduct the complex hearings that deal with unfair labor practices.

Mediators. Their task, as described in chapter 16, is to help labor and management voluntarily settle disputes that arise during contract negotiations.

Specialists on Foreign Labor Movements. These experts analyze developments in unionism in other countries, since labor movements abroad often have a strong influence on their governments and thereby can affect American foreign policies. These specialists include labor attachés at American embassies throughout the world and experts based in Washington at the Department of Labor and the Department of State (see chapter 19).

Jobs with Other Organizations

Arbitrators. A number of private attorneys work as arbitrators, making binding decisions in disputes labor and management cannot settle on their own. The largest group works through the American Arbitration Association, which maintains offices throughout the United States.

Journalists. Major newspapers and magazines have writers on their staffs who specialize in reporting and analyzing developments in labor–management relations.

Lawyers. Every major city has one or more law firms that specialize in the intricacies of labor law and serve as advisors to labor or management.

Librarians. Libraries at major universities frequently have labor relations sections staffed by librarians who specialize in publications in this field.

Professors. Men and women with advanced degrees and/or union experience teach courses in labor relations and conduct research at many universities and colleges.

A Partial Listing of Universities and Colleges Which Offer Training in Labor Relations *

Bachelor's Degree in Labor Relations: Loyola University, Los Angeles; State School of Industrial and Labor Relations at Cornell University, Ithaca, N.Y.; St. Martin's College, Olympia, Washington; University of Utah, Salt Lake City.

Courses Which Lead to a Bachelor's Degree in Related Subjects: California Institute of Technology, Pasadena; Massachusetts Institute of Technology, Cambridge; Princeton University, Princeton, N.J.; Purdue University, Lafayette, Ind.; Queen's University, Ontario; University of California at Los Angeles; University of Hawaii, Honolulu; University of Iowa, Iowa City; University of Michigan, Ann Arbor; Wayne State University, Detroit, Mich.

Graduate Degree in Labor Relations: State School of Industrial and Labor Relations at Cornell University, Ithaca, N.Y.; Laval University, Quebec; Loyola University, Chicago; Michigan State University, East Lansing, Mich.; University of Illinois, Urbana and Chicago; University of Montreal; University of Oregon, Eugene; University of Utah, Salt Lake City; University of Wisconsin, Madison; West Virginia University, Morgantown.

° From data gathered by Julius Rezler, *Industrial and Labor Relations Review,* January, 1968.

TERMS USED IN LABOR RELATIONS *

AFL–CIO. American Federation of Labor–Congress of Industrial Organizations.

African–American Labor Center. See *American Institute for Free
Labor Development.*

Agency shop. See *union security agreements.*

American Institute for Free Labor Development (AIFLD). An organization operated by the AFL–CIO, largely with Federal funds, which en-
courages the development of democratically oriented unions in Central and
South America and opposes the spread of unions dominated by Communist
influences. The AFL–CIO also operates the African–American Labor Center and the Asian–American Free Labor Institute, which have the same
objectives in Africa and Asia (see chapter 19).

---

* These explanations derive from a wide variety of sources. However, my
principal debt is to two detailed manuals: *Industrial and Labor Relations
Terms,* compiled by Robert E. Doherty of the New York State School of Industrial and Labor Relations, and *Speaking of Unions,* published by the International Labor Press Association.

Arbitration. A method of settling a disagreement between a union and an employer over a job grievance or the interpretation of a clause in their contract. A neutral third party—an *arbitrator*—evaluates the arguments, then renders a verdict both sides accept. In a number of cases both also agree to rely on arbitration to settle disputes in contract negotiations. However, compulsory arbitration of such disputes is not used to any extent in the United States, although it is accepted practice in a number of countries (see chapter 16; also see *mediation*).

Asian–American Free Labor Institute. See *American Institute for Free Labor Development*.

Bargaining agent. The union that represents a group of employees in bargaining with their employer. See *bargaining unit, certification, recognition*.

Bargaining unit. The employees a union represents, such as production and maintenance workers in a factory; teachers, librarians, and nurses in a school system; or carpenters or plumbers in a city or a county.

Boycott. A tactic used by a union to force an employer to grant concessions. In a *primary boycott* a union urges consumers not to buy a company's products or use its services until it agrees to raise wages, grants recognition to a new local union, or makes other changes. In a *secondary boycott* the target is a firm that distributes products from the company with which a union has a dispute.

Business agent. An officer of a local union, often a craft union, who manages the union's daily affairs and is paid a salary for his services.

Central Labor Council, Central Labor Union. A federation of local unions in a city or a county which represents the labor movement at the local level.

Certification. The process through which a government certifies a union as bargaining agent after a group of workers select it as their representative.

Checkoff. A system under which union dues are withheld from a worker's pay each month, then turned over to his union.

Closed shop. See *union security agreements*.

Collective bargaining. Negotiations between one or more labor unions and one or more employers over wages, hours, and other conditions of employment. Ordinarily the result is a contract by which both parties agree to abide for a specified period, typically one to four years.

Committeeman. See *shop steward*.

Conciliation. See *mediation*.

Craft union. A union in which membership is restricted to persons with a particular skill.

Fact-finding. See *mediation*.

Featherbedding. Practices demanded by unions and agreed to by employers to prevent the loss of jobs by union members. These include paying for work that is not needed or not performed and deferring installation of automatic, labor-saving equipment.

Federation. An organization of labor unions which speaks for the labor movement at the national, state, or local level. See *AFL–CIO, Central Labor Council.*

Fringe benefits. Insurance, pensions, time off for holidays and vacations, and other benefits paid for by an employer.

Goon. A hoodlum hired by management or labor during a dispute to intimidate the other side.

Grievance. A complaint a worker, a union, or a manager has concerning violation of a work practice or a contract provision. If the two sides cannot reach agreement, most contracts provide that an arbitrator settle the dispute. See *arbitration.*

Hot cargo. Goods shipped from a plant where there is a labor dispute. In some cases unionized workers can refuse to handle or use such goods.

ICFTU. The International Confederation of Free Trade Unions, a global organization of 120 labor federations from non-Communist countries. See *WFTU.*

ILO. The International Labour Organization, an agency of the United Nations which strives to improve economic conditions for workers throughout the world, particularly in newly developing nations.

Industrial union. A union that represents all the employees, skilled and unskilled, in a work place.

Injunction. A court order that prohibits a union or an employer from taking actions a judge believes will unduly injure the other party or the public. For example, injunctions have been used to stop strikes by public employees.

International representative. An employee of an international union who helps local unions negotiate contracts, deal with grievances, and handle other problems. He also may help unorganized workers form local unions. See *organizer.*

International union. A national union which includes local unions outside the United States, particularly in Canada and Puerto Rico. However, all national unions traditionally are referred to as internationals even when their membership is restricted to the United States. See *local union.*

Job action. Since government employees generally do not have the right to strike, many rely on job action to force their employers to grant concessions. Ordinarily a job action involves a slowdown. Workers achieve less, refuse to perform certain duties, and develop "illnesses" which keep a sizable number home each day. When police become ill under such circumstances the disease they contract often is referred to as "blue flu." See *slowdown.*

Local union. A branch of an international union in a particular work place or community.

Lockout. See *strike.*

Maintenance of membership agreement. See *union security agreements.*

Mediation. Also referred to as *conciliation.* This is the principal method in the United States of settling disputes in contract negotiations between unions and employers. A neutral third party, usually a government mediator, tries to help the two sides reach a compromise through techniques discussed in chapter 16. If mediation fails, ordinarily a strike results. If the dispute is of widespread importance, however, the two sides may turn to *fact-finding* in search of a peaceful solution. Typically a government appoints one or more fact-finders who through research try to determine the basic causes of the dispute, then recommend a solution. If the recommendation is rejected, the workers strike or the dispute is submitted to an *arbitrator.* See *arbitration.*

Open shop. See *union security agreements.*

Organizer. A staff member of an international union or the AFL–CIO who helps unorganized workers form local unions. See *international representative.*

Picketing. A demonstration union members use during a strike or some other dispute to dramatize their cause, persuade other workers to join them, and discourage customers from doing business with their employer. Traditionally pickets patrol in front of their work place bearing signs that explain their side of the dispute. Some also resort to *mass picketing,* in which they block entrances to a building by crowding together. Others conduct *informational picketing* at department stores, through which they urge shoppers not to purchase their employer's products.

Raiding. An effort by one international union to capture control of a local union organized by another international. AFL–CIO unions have a no-raiding agreement. So do a number of international unions whose areas of activity overlap. However, raiding persists.

Recognition. An agreement through which an employer formally recognizes a newly formed union as the bargaining agent for his employees. See *bargaining agent, bargaining unit, certification.*

Right-to-Work laws. See *union security agreements.*

Scab. A worker who refuses to join other workers in a strike. Also a strikebreaker who fills the job of a striking worker. See *strike.*

Secondary boycott. See *boycott.*

Seniority. An employee's relative length of service in a job. Most contracts between unions and employers require that employees with the longest service, or the greatest seniority, be given preference in promotions. When cutbacks in staff are necessary, they also must be given preference in the order in which workers are laid off and rehired.

Shop committee. A committee in a local union which deals with problems on the job, often with the help of an international representative. See *shop steward.*

Shop steward, union steward. An officer of a local union who handles grievances for workers in his department and, if there is no checkoff, also collects dues. Frequently management permits him to take time from his work to perform these duties. It even may pay him his salary during these periods. Otherwise, his union reimburses him. He also is known as a *committeeman,* since together with other shop stewards, he is a member of the shop committee. See *shop committee.*

Slowdown. A tactic through which workers reduce the speed at which they do their jobs to win concessions from management. See *job action.*

Speed-up. A situation in which workers are required to produce more, without being paid more.

Stretch-out. A situation in which workers are given extra duties without being paid more.

Strike. A work stoppage to win concessions from an employer. A strike may be used to force management to agree to contract terms a union seeks, to settle a grievance, or to recognize a union as a bargaining agent. Traditionally members of a local union vote on whether to strike, then seek permission of their international union to do so. Workers not directly involved may express their support by walking off their jobs in a *sympathy strike.* In addition, an incident on the job may trigger a spontaneous walkout called a *wildcat strike.* When an employer closes down to force a settlement on his terms, his action is called a *lockout.* See *scab.*

Strikebreaker. See *scab.*

Sweetheart contract. An inferior contract negotiated between a corrupt employer and a corrupt union leader who, for his cooperation, receives a payoff. See *collective bargaining.*

Sympathy strike. See *strike.*

Trustee. If a local union is mismanaged, its international may appoint a temporary trustee to operate the union until its difficulties are straightened out.

Unfair labor practices. Actions by unions or employers which violate Federal or state laws designed to protect their rights. Under Federal law, for example, an employer who fires a worker for joining a union commits an unfair labor practice. So does a union that forces an employer to discriminate against workers who refuse to join.

Union label. A label attached to or imprinted on a product which identifies it as one made by unionized workers. Unionists who perform services, such as barbers and beauticians, may display cards bearing such a label.

Union security agreements. Agreements with management designed to maintain the strength of a local union. Since the law requires that a union represent everyone in its bargaining unit, even the minority who voted against it, labor leaders feel everyone should join or at least pay a fee for the services they receive. At one point unions were able to win a *closed shop* agreement under which an employer had to hire union members, but, when this was declared illegal, unions sought other arrangements. Four types of union security agreements currently are negotiated, varying with a union's bargaining power and an employer's strength:

A *union shop:* All employees in a bargaining unit must join the union after a specified period, usually thirty to ninety days.

Preferential hiring: In adding employees, an employer must give preference to union members.

Maintenance of membership: Workers may join a union or not. But those who join must remain members for the duration of the current contract. If they decide to drop their membership, they may do so only during a two-week period each year.

An agency shop: Workers may join a union or not. But those who do not join must pay a monthly fee to reimburse the union for negotiating contracts, handling grievances, and other services.

As discussed in chapter 7, union security agreements are banned in nineteen states, primarily in rural areas. Each has a *right-to-work law* which requires an *open shop.* Under this arrangement employees need not join unions nor pay service fees to keep their jobs.

Union shop. See *union security agreements.*

WFTU. The World Federation of Trade Unions, a global organization of forty labor federations from Communist countries and other nations where a labor federation has close ties with the Communist Party. See *ICFTU.*

Wildcat strike. See *strike.*

Work rules. Since these regulate working conditions, usually they are part of the contract a union and an employer negotiate. Some are designed to protect workers from arbitrary action by employers. Others are designed to preserve management's rights to make final decisions in scheduling, the use of new techniques, and related matters.

BIBLIOGRAPHY AND SUGGESTED READINGS

The publications listed below were among my primary resources. A number of them are of a technical nature, but many will be of interest to teachers and students who wish to learn more about unions and labor–management relations. Those publications preceded by an asterisk (°) may have particular appeal for students.

Surveys of the Labor Movement, Discussion of Contemporary Problems

° Allen, Steve. *The Ground Is Our Table*. New York: Doubleday & Co., 1966
Bakke, Edward W., *et al. Unions, Management, and the Public*. New York: Harcourt, Brace & World, 1960.
Barbash, Jack. *American Unions*. New York: Random House, 1967.
———. *Labor's Grass Roots*. New York: Harper & Row, 1961.

————. *Unions and Union Leadership.* New York: Harper & Row, 1959.

Bloom, Gordon, *et al. Economics of Labor Relations.* Homewood, Illinois: Richard D. Irwin, Inc., 1958.

° Boardman, Fon W. *Economics: Ideas and Men.* New York: H. Z. Walck, 1966.

Bok, Derek, and Dunlop, John. *Labor and the American Community.* New York: Simon and Schuster, 1970.

Brooke, Milton, *et al. Growth of Labor Law in the United States.* Washington, D.C.: U.S. Department of Labor, 1967.

Chamberlain, Neil. *Labor.* New York: McGraw–Hill Book Co., 1958.

° Cullen, Donald E. *Negotiating Labor–Management Contracts.* Ithaca, N.Y.: New York State School of Industrial and Labor Relations, 1965.

———— and Greenberg, Marcia L. *Management Rights and Collective Bargaining.* Ithaca, N.Y.: New York State School of Industrial and Labor Relations, 1966.

Directory of National and International Labor Unions in the United States. Washington, D.C.: Bureau of Labor Statistics, U.S. Department of Labor, 1970.

° Ellis, Harry B. *Ideas and Ideologies.* New York and Cleveland: The World Publishing Co., 1968.

° Estey, Martin S., *et al. Regulating Union Government.* New York: Harper & Row, 1964.

Farm Labor Organizing, 1905–1967. New York: National Advisory Committee on Farm Labor, 1967.

Greenhill, H. Gaylon. *Labor Money in Wisconsin Politics, 1964.* Princeton, N.J.: Citizens' Research Foundation, 1964.

° Greenstone, J. David. *Labor in American Politics.* New York: Alfred A. Knopf, 1969.

° Gregory, Charles O. *Labor and the Law.* New York: W. W. Norton, 1961.

° Hirsch, S. Carl. *This Is Automation.* New York: The Viking Press, 1964.

° Hume, A. Britton. *Death and the Mines: Rebellion and Murder in the UMW.* New York: Grossman Publishers, 1971.

Hutchinson, John. *The Imperfect Union: A History of Corruption in American Trade Unions.* New York: E. P. Dutton & Co., 1970.

Jacobs, Paul. *Dead Horse and Featherbed.* Santa Barbara, Calif.: Center for the Study of Democratic Institutions, 1962.

————. *Old Before Its Time: Collective Bargaining at 28.* Santa Barbara, Calif.: Center for the Study of Democratic Institutions, 1963.

° Jacobson, Julius, ed. *The Negro and the American Labor Movement.* New York: Doubleday & Co., 1968.

Labor Looks at Labor. Santa Barbara, Calif.: Center for the Study of Democratic Institutions, 1963.

Marshall, F. Ray. *The Negro and Organized Labor.* New York: John Wiley & Sons, Inc., 1965.

Moscow, Michael S. *et al. Collective Bargaining in Public Employment.* New York: Random House, 1970.

Perry, Charles R., and Wildman, Wisby. *The Impact of Negotiations in Public Education.* Worthington, Ohio: Charles A. Jones Publishing Co., 1970.

° Peterson, Florence. *American Labor Unions.* New York: Harper & Row, 1963.

° Samuelson, Paul A. *Economics.* 8th ed. New York: McGraw–Hill Book Co., 1970.

° Seidman, Joel, *et al. The Worker Views His Union.* Chicago: University of Chicago Press, 1958.

° Soule, George H. *The New Science of Economics, an Introduction.* New York: The Viking Press, 1964.

° Sultan, Paul E. *The Disenchanted Unionist.* New York: Harper & Row, 1963.

° Walsh, Robert E., ed. *Sorry. . . . No Government Today: Unions vs. City Hall.* Boston: Beacon Press, 1969.

Windmuller, John P. *The Foreign Policy Conflict in American Labor.* Ithaca, N.Y.: New York State School of Labor and Industrial Relations, 1967.

———. *International Trade Union Organizations.* Ithaca, N.Y.: New York State School of Labor and Industrial Relations, 1967.

History and Biography

° Bernstein, Irving. *The Lean Years: A History of the American Worker, 1920–1933.* Boston: Houghton Mifflin Co., 1960.

° ———. *The Turbulent Years, 1933–1941.* Boston: Houghton Mifflin Co., 1970.

° Bird, Caroline. *The Invisible Scar.* New York: David McKay Co., 1966.

° *Brief History of the American Labor Movement.* Washington, D.C.: Bulletin 1000, Superintendent of Documents.

° Brooks, Thomas R. *Toil and Trouble.* New York: Delacorte Press, 1964.

° Chaplin, Ralph. *Wobbly: The Rough and Tumble Story of an American Radical.* Chicago: University of Chicago Press, 1948.

° Cooke, Donald E. *The Romance of Capitalism.* New York: Holt, Rinehart and Winston, 1968.

° Cormier, Frank, and Eaton, William J. *Reuther.* Englewood, N.J.: Prentice–Hall, 1970.

° Daniels, Patricia. *Famous Labor Leaders.* New York: Dodd Mead & Co., 1970.

° Dubofsky, Melvyn. *We Shall Be All: A History of the Industrial Workers of the World.* Chicago: Quadrangle Books, 1969.

Dulles, Foster R. *Labor in America.* New York: Thomas Y. Crowell, 1966.
° Gurko, Miriam. *Clarence Darrow.* New York: Thomas Y. Crowell, 1965.
° Josephson, Matthew. *Sidney Hillman: Statesman of American Labor.* New York: Doubleday & Co., 1952.
° Kennedy, Robert F. *The Enemy Within.* New York: Harper & Row, 1960.
° Kornbluh, Joyce L., ed. *Rebel Voices: An I.W.W. Anthology.* Ann Arbor, Mich.: University of Michigan Press, 1968.
° Lewis, Arthur H. *Lament for the Molly Maguires.* New York: Harcourt, Brace & World, 1964.
Lynd, Staughton, ed. *Non-Violence in America.* Indianapolis and New York: Bobbs–Merrill Co., 1965.
° Matthiessen, Peter. *Sal Si Puedes—Escape If You Can: Cesar Chavez and the New American Revolution.* New York: Random House, 1970.
° Meltzer, Milton. *Bread—and Roses: The Struggle of American Labor, 1865–1915.* New York: Alfred A. Knopf, 1967.
° Paradis, Adrian A. *The Hungry Years: The Story of the Great American Depression.* Philadelphia: Chilton Co., 1967.
° Pelling, Henry. *American Labor.* Chicago: University of Chicago Press, 1960.
° Perlman, Selig. *History of Trade Unionism in the United States.* New York: A. M. Kelley, 1922.
Rayback, Joseph A. *History of American Labor.* New York: Macmillan Co., 1961.
Schlesinger, Arthur M., Jr. *The Coming of the New Deal.* Boston: Houghton Mifflin Co., 1958.
° Selden, David F. *Champions of Labor.* New York: Abelard–Schuman, 1967.
° ——. *Eugene Debs.* New York: Lothrop, Lee & Shepard, 1966.
° ——. *Samuel Gompers.* New York: Abelard–Schuman, 1964.
° Stein, Leon. *The Triangle Fire.* Philadelphia: J. B. Lippincott, 1967.
Taft, Philip. *Organized Labor in American History.* New York: Harper & Row, 1964.
° Werstein, Irving. *The Great Struggle.* New York: Charles Scribner's Sons, 1965.
° Wright, Dale. *They Harvest Despair.* Boston: Beacon Press, 1965.

Fiction

° Dos Passos, John. *Midcentury.* Boston: Houghton Mifflin Co., 1961.
° Field, Rachel L. *And Now Tomorrow.* New York: Macmillan Co., 1942.
° Gates, Doris. *Blue Willow.* New York: The Viking Press, 1940.
° Hobson, Laura Z. *First Papers.* New York: Random House, 1964.

* Hulbert, James. *Noon on the Third Day*. New York: Holt, Rinehart and Winston, 1962.
* Johnson, Annabel, and E. *Bearcat*. New York: Harper & Row, 1960.
* Llewellyn, Richard. *How Green Was My Valley*. New York: Macmillan Co., 1940.
* Shotwell, Louisa R. *Roosevelt Grady*. New York and Cleveland: The World Publishing Co., 1963.
* Sinclair, Upton. *The Jungle*. New York: Dial Press, 1906.
* Steinbeck, John. *Grapes of Wrath*. New York: The Viking Press, 1939.
* Stone, Irving. *Adversary in the House*. New York: Doubleday & Co., 1947.
* Young, Bob, and Jan. *Goodbye, Amigos*. New York: Julian Messner, 1963.

Periodicals

American Federationist, AFL–CIO, 815 Sixteenth Street NW, Washington, D.C. 20026. A partisan approach.
American Labor, the Magazine of Labor News, 444 Madison Avenue, New York, N.Y. 10022
Business Week, 330 W. 42d Street, New York, N.Y. 10036. Particularly the section on labor–management relations.
Canadian Labour, Canadian Labour Congress, 100 Argyle Avenue, Ottawa 4, Ontario, Canada. A partisan approach.
Industrial Relations, Institute of Industrial Relations, University of California, Berkeley, Calif. 94720
Industrial and Labor Relations Review, New York State School of Industrial and Labor Relations, Cornell University, Ithaca, N.Y. 14850
Labor History, Taminent Institute, 7 E. 15th Street, New York, N.Y. 10003
Monthly Labor Review, Superintendent of Documents, U.S. Government Printing Office, Washington, D.C. 20402
New York Times, 229 W. 43rd Street, New York, N.Y. 10036

Free or Inexpensive Materials on Labor Relations

PUBLICATIONS
Lists are available from the following sources:

Government

Superintendent of Documents, Washington, D.C. 20402
Bureau of Labor Statistics, 441 G Street NW, Washington, D.C. 20001

U.S. Federal Mediation and Conciliation Service, Department of Labor Building, Washington, D.C. 20427

Women's Bureau, U.S. Department of Labor, Washington, D.C. 20210

International Labour Organization, Public Information Division, 917 Fifteenth Street NW, Washington, D.C. 20005

Individual state departments of labor.

Private Agency

American Arbitration Association, 140 W. 51st Street, New York, N.Y. 10019

Universities

University of California, Institute of Industrial Relations, 210 California Hall, Berkeley, Calif. 94720

University of California, Institute of Industrial Relations, 405 Hilgard Avenue, Los Angeles, Calif. 90024

University of Chicago, Industrial Relations Center, 1225 E. 60th Street, Chicago, Ill. 60637

Cornell University, New York State School of Industrial and Labor Relations, Ives Hall, Ithaca, N.Y. 14850; 7 E. 43d Street, New York, N.Y. 10017

University of Illinois, Institute of Labor and Industrial Relations, 704 S. 6th Street, Champaign, Ill. 61820

University of Iowa, Center for Labor and Management, 24 Phillips Hall, Iowa City, Iowa 52240

University of Massachusetts, Labor Research and Relations Center, Amherst, Mass. 01002

University of Michigan, Institute of Labor and Industrial Relations, 403 South Kedzie Hall, East Lansing, Mich. 48823

University of Pennsylvania, Industrial Relations Unit, Wharton School of Finance and Commerce, Philadelphia, Pa. 19104

Rutgers, The State University, Institute of Management and Labor Relations, Ryders Lane and Clifton Avenue, New Brunswick, N.J. 08903

Wayne State University, Institute of Labor and Industrial Relations, 5229 Cass Avenue, Detroit, Mich. 48202

Business Organizations   (partisan materials)

Chamber of Commerce of the United States, 1615 H Street NW, Washington, D.C. 20006

Committee for Economic Development, 711 Fifth Avenue, New York, N.Y. 10022

E. I. duPont de Nemours and Company, Wilmington, Del. 19801

Ford Motor Company, 3000 Schaefer Road, Dearborn, Mich. 48121

General Electric Company, 570 Lexington Avenue, New York, N.Y. 10022

National Association of Manufacturers, Education Department, 277 Park Avenue, New York, N.Y. 10017

National Industrial Conference Board, Inc., 460 Park Avenue, New York, N.Y. 10022

United States Steel Corporation, Public Relations Department, 600 Grant Street, Pittsburgh, Pa. 15219

Individual state chambers of commerce and manufacturers associations.

Labor Organizations (partisan materials)

Amalgamated Clothing Workers of America, 14 Union Square, New York, N.Y. 10003

Amalgamated Meat Cutters and Butcher Workmen of North America, 2800 North Sheridan Road, Chicago, Ill. 60657

American Federation of Labor and Congress of Industrial Organizations, AFL–CIO Building, 815 Sixteenth Street NW, Washington, D.C. 20006

American Federation of Labor and Congress of Industrial Organizations, Industrial Union Department, 815 Sixteenth Street NW, Washington, D.C. 20006

International Association of Machinists, 1300 Connecticut Avenue NW, Washington, D.C. 20036

International Brotherhood of Electrical Workers, 1200 Fifteenth Street NW, Washington, D.C. 20005

International Brotherhood of Teamsters, Chauffeurs, Warehousemen and Helpers of America, 25 Louisiana Avenue NW, Washington, D.C. 20001

International Chemical Workers Union, 1659 West Market Street, Akron, Ohio 44313

International Ladies' Garment Workers' Union, 1710 Broadway, New York, N.Y. 20019

International Union of Electrical, Radio, and Machine Workers, 1126 Sixteenth Street NW, Washington, D.C. 20036

International Union of United Automobile, Aerospace and Agricultural Implement Workers of America, 8000 East Jefferson Avenue, Detroit, Mich. 48214

La Causa Distribution Center of Chicano Materials, 1516 34th Avenue, Oakland, Calif. 94601

Oil, Chemical and Atomic Workers International Union, P.O. Box 2812, Denver, Colo. 80202

Retail, Wholesale and Department Store Union, 132 West 43d Street, New York, N.Y. 10036

Textile Workers Union of America, 99 University Place, New York, N.Y. 10003

United Brotherhood of Carpenters and Joiners of America, 222 East Michigan Avenue, Indianapolis, Ind. 46204

FILMS

There are scores of films and other audio-visual materials on the labor movement and labor relations which may be rented, and in some cases may be obtained free, from unions, universities, state and public libraries, and commercial organizations. A primary source of information is the Educational Film Library Association, 17 West 60th Street, New York, N.Y. 10023. One of the most complete national sources of films on unionism is the AFL–CIO Film Library, 815 16th Street NW, Washington, D.C. 20006. A sampling of key regional sources is listed below. Ordinarily catalogues are provided on request.

Arizona University of Arizona, Bureau of Audio-Visual Services, Tucson, Ariz. 85721

California University of California Extension Media Center, Berkeley, Calif. 94720

Canada Canadian Film Institute, 1762 Carling, Ottawa 13, Ontario, Canada. Metropolitan Toronto Library Board, 124 College Street, Toronto 13, Ontario, Canada

Colorado Colorado State College, Instructional Materials Center, Greeley, Colo. 80631

Connecticut University of Connecticut Audio-Visual Center, Storrs, Conn. 06268

Georgia University of Georgia Center for Continuing Education, 16mm Library, Athens, Ga. 30601

Illinois University of Illinois, Division of University Extension, Visual Aids Service, Champaign, Ill. 61820

Indiana Indiana University Audio-Visual Center, Division of University Extension, Bloomington, Ind. Particularly *The Union Man* and *The Labor Movement—Beginnings and Growth in America.*

Iowa University of Iowa, Division of Extension and University Services, Audio-Visual Center, Iowa City, Iowa 52240

Massachusetts Boston University Film Department, 765 Commonwealth Avenue, Boston, Mass. 02215

Michigan Michigan State University, Instructional Media Center, East Lansing, Mich. 44823. University of Michigan Audio-Visual Center, Frieze

Building, Ann Arbor, Mich. 48104. Wayne State University, Audio-Visual Utilization Center, 5448 Cass Avenue, Detroit, Mich. 48202

New Hampshire University of New Hampshire, Audio-Visual Center, Durham, N.H. 03824

New York New York University Film Library, 26 Washington Place, New York, N.Y. 10003. Syracuse University Film Library, 1455 East Colvin Street, Syracuse, N.Y. 13210

Pennsylvania Pennsylvania State University, Audio-Visual Materials, University Park, Pa. 16802

Texas University of Texas, Visual Instruction Bureau, Austin, Tex. 78712

Utah Brigham Young University, Department of Audio-Visual Communication, Provo, Utah 84601

INDEX

Administrator of labor laws, 241
AFL, *see* American Federation of Labor
AFL–CIO, *see* American Federation of Labor–Congress of Industrial Organizations
African-American Labor Center, 230
AFSCME, *see* American Federation of State, County, and Municipal Employees
Agency shop, 95
AIFLD, *see* American Institute for Free Labor Development
Air Line Pilots Associations, 88
Alliance for Labor Action, 67
Amalgamated Clothing Workers, 29, 50, 86, 88, 114
Amalgamated Meat Cutters and

Butcher Workmen, Local 80A of, 91–92
American Airlines, 114
American Arbitration Association, 242
American Farm Bureau, 78
American Federation of Government Employees, 70
American Federation of Labor, 44, 45, 47, 48, 50, 51, 58, 60
American Federation of Labor–Congress of Industrial Organizations, 27, 60, 61, 63, 64, 75, 97, 113, 115, 116, 121, 124, 127, 133, 155, 224, 226, 229, 240; code of ethics adopted by, 124; Communism opposed by, 64, 221; and COPE, 214, 216,

American Federation of Labor (Cont.)
217; Department of International Relations of, 221; Education Department of, 239; Executive Council of, 63; Film Library of, 257; goals of, 64; lobbying by, 219, 220, 221; member unions of, 64, 65; political activities by, 107, 214, 216; reports of, on Congressmen's votes, 214, 215; structures of, 65, 66

American Federation of State, County, and Municipal Employees, 69–72, 81, 81 n, 210, 231, 232

American Federation of Teachers, 70, 88, 155, 211; Local 2 of, 92–93

American Institute for Free Labor Development, 229, 230, 231

American Machine and Foundry Company, 207

Arbitration, 104, 198–99, 200, 210, 242

Argentina, 225

Asia, 225, 229

Asian-American Free Labor Institute, 230

Audio-visual materials, on labor movement, 257–58

Australia, unions in, 200, 224

Authorization cards, 160, 161, 162

Automation, 182, 183, 184, 195

Bakery Workers Union, 94, 124

Ballot, used by NLRB, 167

Baltimore & Ohio Railroad, 40

Bargaining, collective, see Collective bargaining

Bargaining unit, represented by local union, 95

Baseball Players Association, 88, 177

Bass, Ross, 217

Beck, Dave, 122, 123

Birkholz, Ray, 165

Black Thursday (Oct. 24, 1929), 48

Blacks: and civil rights, 222; as strikebreakers, 116; and unions, 91, 97, 98, 115, 117, 118, 119, 215

Boilermakers Union, 117

Boycott, secondary, 140

Boyle, Tony, 82, 83, 84

British Guiana (Guyana), 231, 232

Brotherhood of Sleeping Car Porters, 116

Bureau of Labor Statistics, U.S., 239, 241

Bustamente, Alexander, 226

Byrne, Joseph, 80

Campbell Soup Company, 91

Canada, 27 n, 200

Canadian Labor Congress, 224

Carpenters Union, 28, 88, 117; Local 781 of, 90, 91

Castro, Fidel, 229

Caucus, in contract negotiation, 193

Central Intelligence Agency, 230–31

Chamber of Commerce, U.S., 124, 134, 144

Chavez, Cesar, 73, 74, 75, 77, 78

Checkoff, 88

Child labor, 39, 42, 43

Chile, 225

Chrysler Corporation, 55

CIA, see Central Intelligence Agency

Cigar Makers Union, 28, 44

CIO, see Congress of Industrial Organizations

CISC, see International Confederation of Christian Trade Unions

Civil Rights Act (1964), 116

Civil War, 38, 40

Closed shop, 95, 140

Cold war, 225, 228, 229

Collective bargaining, 28, 31, 102, 172–200; bluffing and haggling in, 191; continuous, 194–95; coordinated, 188; fact-finding in, 198; fringe benefits through, 175–80; and government employees, 188–209; ground rules for, 189–90; industry-wide, 187; issues in, 172–85; and job security, 180, 181, 182; and mediation, 196–98, 242; pay increases through, 173–75; *see also* Contract, negotiation of

Committee on Political Education, 214, 216, 217

Communications Workers, 80, 114

Communism, 58, 64, 67, 213, 222, 225, 228

Community Health Association of Detroit, 86

Company unions, 48, 49

Congress of Industrial Organizations, 51, 55, 56, 58

Construction industries, local unions of, 91, 214

Contract, negotiation of, 189–91, 193–98; *see also* Collective bargaining

Coolidge, Calvin, 209

"Cooling off" period, eighty-day, 198

Cooperatives, 38, 42, 44

COPE, *see* Committee on Political Education

CORE, 76

Cornell University, 143, 242, 243

Corruption, in unions, 120 ff

Craft unions, 28, 44, 50, 85, 97, 102, 106

Curran, Joseph, 82

Davis, Leon, 119

Day-care centers, on agenda of labor lobby, 222

Deering Millikin & Company, 171

Democratic Party, 213, 214, 217, 219

Department of Labor, U.S., 85, 136, 239, 242

Depression, Great, 73, 137

Detroit Musicians Union, 53

Directory of National and International Unions in the United States, 239

Drug and Hospital Union, Local 1199 of, 118–19

Education and Labor Committee, in House of Representatives, 241

England, unions in, 223, 224, 225

Farm Workers union, 28

FBI, *see* Federal Bureau of Investigation

Featherbedding, 182

Federal government, 135–42, 148, 188; mediation by, 196–98, 242

Federal Mediation and Conciliation Service, 136, 195, 239

Federal Society of Journeyman Cordwainers, 37

Ford Motor Company, 55, 229

Foreman, 103

France, unions in, 224, 225

Fringe benefits, 175–80

General Electric Company, 22, 23, 24, 51, 188, 202

General Motors Corporation, 51, 52, 53, 187

Glass Blowers union, 132

Gompers, Samuel, 44, 48, 145, 153, 172, 213

Gould, Jay, 43, 44

Government: employees of, and collective bargaining, 188, 209; Federal, *see* Federal government; jobs with, in regulating labor-

Government (Cont.)
management relations, 241–42;
strikes against, 207–10
Grape boycott, 77–78
Grapes of Wrath, The (Steinbeck),
73
Green, William, 48, 58, 65
Greenback-Laborites, 213
Grievance system, 102, 104, 132,
181
Guimarra Vineyards, 77, 78
Guinan, Matthew, 80
Guinea, 226

Hall, Paul, 80
Hamilton Watch Company, 173
Hanna, Tadgh, 207, 210
Hat Finishers union, 38
Haynsworth, Clement F., 220
Haywood, "Big Bill," 45
Health insurance: labor-management
negotiations on, 176, 177; na-
tional, 222
Hillman, Sidney, 29
Hiring halls, 102
Hoffa, James R., 29, 120, 122, 123,
144, 145
Hotel and Restaurant Workers, 114
House of Representatives, U.S., 136,
216, 241
Huerta, Dolores, 74, 75, 77
Humphrey, Hubert, 217

IAM, *see* International Association
of Machinists
ICFTU, *see* International Confed-
eration of Free Trade Unions
Industrial Revolution, 40
Industrial unions, 28
Industrial Workers of the World
(Wobblies), 45–47, 51
Inflation, 22, 83, 174, 175, 176
Insurance, labor-management nego-
tiations on, 175, 176, 177

International Association of Fire
Fighters, 70
International Association of Ma-
chinists, 31, 68–69, 133, 157
International Brotherhood of Team-
sters, 28, 28 n, 29, 30, 31, 58,
65, 67, 80, 85; corruption in,
121–23; expelled from AFL–CIO,
124
International Chemical Workers
Union, 162
International Confederation of Chris-
tian Trade Unions, 228
International Confederation of Free
Trade Unions, 228, 229
International Ladies' Garment
Workers Union, 29, 86, 218
International Longshoremen's As-
sociation, 58
International Typographical Union,
38, 81
International union(s), 27, 27 n, 28,
29, 30, 64, 65, 66, 68, 79–89,
113, 116, 157; jobs with, 240–
41; locals organized by, 154,
155; *see also* Collective bar-
gaining; Contract, negotiation of;
Labor relations
Iowa Beef Processors, 206
Iron Workers Union, 117
Israel, unions in, 224
Italy, 175; general strike in, 226–
27; unions in, 224, 225, 226–27

Jamaica, 226
Japan, unions in, 224
Job security, 180, 181, 182
John Birch Society, 78
Johnson, Lyndon B., 63

Kaiser Steel Company, 184, 195
Kaven, William H., 146
Kennedy, John F., 217, 231, 232
Kennedy, Robert F., 122, 124
Kenya, 223, 226

Kilroy, Thomas, 56
King, Martin Luther, Jr., 72, 96, 119
Knights of Labor, 42, 43, 44, 45
Kohler Company, 202

Labor and Public Welfare Committee, in U.S. Senate, 241
Labor Day, 34, 212
Labor Department, U.S., 85, 136, 239, 242
Labor-Management Services Administration, 136, 239
Labor relations: bachelor's degree in, 242; careers in, 239–42; and Federal government, 135–41, 241–42; graduate degree in, 243; list of schools offering training in, 242–43; specialist in, 241; and states, 141–42; *see also* Management; Union(s)
Labour Party, British, 225
Landrum-Griffin(Labor-Management Reporting and Disclosure) Act (1959), 124, 140, 149
Latin America, 225, 229, 230
Laundry Workers union, 124
Letter Carriers union, 70 n
Lewis, John L., 50, 52, 56, 57, 65, 82
Linotype operators, in make-work arrangements, 184
Little Steel, 55, 56, 57
Lobby, labor, 219–22
Local union(s), 27, 61, 66, 90–109; as bargaining agent, 94, 95, 159; and grievance system, 102, 104; help by, with members' personal problems, 106–7; and illustrative cases of job disputes, 104–6, 108–9; law of, 100–101; meetings of, 99, 100; members of, 98, 99–100, 106–7 (*see also* Rank and file); officials

of, 97–98, 99, 100, 101; political involvement of, 107; and racial discrimination, 91, 97, 115, 116, 117, 118; as seedbed of unionism, 93–97; and union-security agreements, 95, 96; *see also* Collective bargaining; Contract, negotiation of; Labor relations
Lockout, 191, 195
Locomotive Engineers union, 38
Loudon, Tenn., election at, 162–67

McClellan Committee, 122, 124
MacDonald, David, 82
McKinney, Ernest Rice, 146, 147
Mafia, 120, 125, 126
Management, 131–34, 147, 148, 149, 172
Massachusetts, Supreme Court of, 38
Mboya, Tom, 226
Meany, George, 58, 59, 60, 145
Mediators, Federal, 196–98, 242
Memorial Day Massacre (1937), 54, 56
Mexican-Americans, 73, 206; and unions, 97
Morrison, Harold, 21
Murphy, Frank, 52, 53
Murray, Philip, 56, 58, 60, 65
Musicians union, 88

National Association of Manufacturers, 124, 134, 141
National Bank of Washington, 88
National Council of Distributive Workers of America, 118
National Education Association, 70, 155
National Farm Workers Association, 74, 75
National Labor Relations Board, 136,

National Labor Relations Board (Cont.)
138, 139, 141, 162, 167, 170, 171, 180, 239, 240, 242
National Maritime Union, 82, 86
National Mediation Board, 136
National Organization for Women, 115
National Right to Work Committee, 78
National Trades Union Council, 37–38
Negotiations, labor-management, *see* Collective bargaining *and* Contract, negotiation of
New York City: Central Labor Council in, 208; Co-op City in, 86, 87; hospital workers in, 118, 119, 173, 191–93; Labor Day parade in, 34; Metropolitan Transit Authority in, 176; racket unions in, 126, 127; sanitation workers' strike in, 208–9, 210; Stock Exchange in, 48; Teachers and Board of Education in, 70; United Federation of Teachers in, 92–93, 107
New Zealand, 200
Newark, teachers' strike in, 210–11
NFWA, *see* National Farm Workers Association
Nixon, Richard, 78, 175, 212, 220
NLRB, *see* National Labor Relations Board
Norris–La Guardia Act (1932), 137–38
NOW, *see* National Organization for Women

Open shop, 95
Organizers, union, 153–71 *passim*, 240

Painters District Council 9, 127–28

Pensions, labor-management negotiations on, 175, 176, 177
Perón, Juan, 225
Picket line, 205; crossing, 204
Plumbers Union, 28, 117
Police strike, Boston (1919), 209
Politics, and labor, 107, 212–22
Postal Clerks Union, 70 n
Presidents, union, 80
Press, union criticism of, 145
Proxmire, William, 216
Public attitudes, and unions, 143–49
Puerto Ricans, and unions, 97, 117, 118, 119
Puerto Rico, 27 n
Purdue University, 144, 242–43

Racket unions, 126–27
Racketeers, 120 ff
Railroad strike (1877), 40–41
Randolph, A. Philip, 116
Rank and file, 110–19; diversity of, 111; and racial minorities, 115–19; women among, 113–15; young people among, 112–13; *see also* Union(s), membership of
Rarback, Martin, 127, 128
Reagan, Ronald, 78
Republic Steel Corporation, 55, 56
Republican Party, 213, 214, 219
Retail, Wholesale, and Department Store Union, 117–18
Retail Clerks Union, 76, 114
Retirement plans, labor-management negotiations on, 176, 177, 178
Reuther, Walter, 29, 59, 60, 145
Right-to-work laws, 96, 97 n
Roosevelt, Franklin D., 53, 216
Ross, Fred, 74, 75
Rubber Workers Union, 28
Russia, 229; unions in, 223, 227
Russian Revolution, 58

Scab (strikebreaker), 116, 203, 206
Schenley Distillers, 76, 77
Schonfeld, Frank, 128
Seafarers International Union, 30, 80, 88, 178
Sears Roebuck and Company, 123–24
Secretary-treasurer, union, 80
Security, job, 180, 181, 182
Senate, U.S., 136, 220, 241
Seniority system, 181
Shanker, Albert, 93
Shop steward, 97, 103, 104
Sit-down strike, 51, 52, 53
Slater, Samuel, 38
"Slot-machine" union member, 112
Social Security, 177, 222
Socialist Party, 213
Solidarity, 89
South Vietnam, union meeting in, 223
Soviet Union, *see* Russia
Spain, unions in, 223
Steelworkers Organizing Committee, 55, 56
Stone Cutters Union, 38
Strike(s), 22–25, 40–42, 57, 58, 147, 148, 159, 190, 199, 200, 201–11; Boston police (1919), 209; general, 226; against General Electric Company, 21–25, 202; against government, 207–10; ground rule for, 190; against Kohler Company, 202–3; postmen's, 207–8, 210; railroad (1877), 40–41; sanitation workers', in Memphis, 71–72; sanitation workers', in New York, 208–9, 210; sit-down, 51, 52, 53; statistics on, 201–2; steel (1919), 116; sympathy, 203, 204; teachers', in New York, 93; teachers', in Newark, 210–11; wildcat, 204

Strike benefits, 205
Strikebreaker (scab), 116, 203, 206
Supreme Court, U.S., 139, 171, 220
Sweden, 175; unions in, 223, 224
"Sweetheart" contract, 126, 127

Taft-Hartley (Labor-Management Relations) Act (1947), 95, 139–40, 148
Teamsters, *see* International Brotherhood of Teamsters
Textile Workers Union, 154, 155, 157, 158, 171
Touré, Sékou, 226
Trades Union Congress, British, 224, 225
Transport Workers Union, 80, 114, 176, 191; Rank and file Workers within, 117

UFWOC, *see* United Farm Workers Organizing Committee
UMW Journal, 83
Union(s), 29, 151; activities of, 85–89, 151, 222; anti-Communism of, 64, 220–21; banks operated by, 88; "bread-and-butter," 85; and checkoff, 88; Communist infiltration of, 58; company, 48, 49; contributions by, to candidates for political office, 216–17; and corruption, 120 ff; craft, 28, 44, 50, 85, 97, 102, 106; educational programs of, 86; foreign, 223–32, 242; future of, 233–35; history of, 35–60, 213; income of, sources of, 88; industrial, 28; international, *see* International union(s); jobs with, 240–41; lobbying by, 219–22; local, *see* Local union(s); and management, *see* Management; membership of, 27, 31, 33, 61, 98–100, 106–7, 110–11, 144,

Union(s) (Cont.)
156 (*see also* Rank and file); membership of, by states, 32–33; officials of, 80; organizing by, 153–71 *passim;* and politics, 107, 212–22; programs of, 85–89, 151, 222; and public, attitudes of, 143–49; and racial discrimination, 91, 97, 115, 116, 117, 118; racket, 126–27; rank and file of, *see* Rank and file; salaries of officials of, 80; solidarity of, 89; *see also* Collective bargaining; Contract, negotiation of; Labor relations
Union Carbide Corporation, 133
Union label, 64, 64 n
Union shop, 95, 149
United Auto Workers, 28, 28 n, 29, 31, 52, 53, 60, 65, 67, 79, 86, 112, 114, 154, 157, 168, 187, 229; Dodge Revolutionary Movement within, 117; Local 502 of, 107; Local 1416 of, 158; Public Review Board of, 101
United Electrical Workers, 31, 67, 114, 117
United Farm Workers Organizing Committee, 72
United Federation of Teachers, 92–93, 107
United Mine Workers, 48, 50, 55, 57, 65, 82, 88
United States Steel Corporation, 55, 133
United Steelworkers, 28, 28 n, 30, 31, 55, 81, 146, 187, 195
United Textile Workers, 155
United Transportation Union, 88
Universities, union criticism of, 145, 146
University of California, 47, 243
University of Virginia, course on unionism at, 146

Upper Volta, 223
Urban League, 116

Vacations, labor-management negotiations on, 175, 178
Venezuela, 229
Vice-presidents, union, 80
Vietnam, 147, 222, 223

Wage-price spiral, 174, 175
Wagner (National Labor Relations) Act (1935), 138, 139, 140, 187
Wallace, George, 117
Washington, D.C.: AFL–CIO school operated in, 154; COPE in, 214; National Bank of, 88
Washington, George, 37
Watch Workers Union, 28
Western Federation of Miners, 45
WFTU, *see* World Federation of Trade Unions
Wildcat strike, 204
Window Cutters Union, 28
Wobblies, *see* Industrial Workers of the World
Women, in labor movement, 113–15
Women's Liberation Movement, 115
Woodcock, Leonard, 79
Work force, changes in, from 1900 through 1970s, 30
Workingmen's Party, 37, 213
Workmen's compensation, 32
World Federation of Trade Unions, 228
World War I, 47
World War II, 57, 176
Wurf, Jerry, 80, 81, 82

Yablonski, Joseph A., 82, 83, 84, 85
"Yellow dog" contract, 47, 137

ABOUT THE AUTHOR

ALVIN SCHWARTZ is a native of New York City. He is a graduate of Colby College and obtained an M.S. degree in journalism from Northwestern University. After graduation he worked as a newspaper reporter and held jobs in public relations and advertising. For several years he was Director of Communications at the Opinion Research Corporation in Princeton, New Jersey.

Since 1964 he has devoted his time to writing for young people on the social sciences and the arts, and for adults on recreational activities. In addition he teaches English on a part-time basis at Rutgers University.

Mr. Schwartz writes: "My serious books are for young people largely because they are the most important audience I know of." *The Unions* is part of a body of work on American institutions and movements which includes *University*, a study of one institution of higher learning.

Mr. Schwartz and his wife and four children make their home in Princeton.